Both Hands for Me

MALIA SIMON

To my grandmother

Entry One

I woke today to the smell of old Band-Aids and dry skin on the backs of my elbows for the first time in years. Whenever I think of the pungent smell of Band-Aids I think of the place I used to live, where I never left myself alone. Always scraping up my knees and wrists doing pointless things in desperate attempt to gain my mother's attention, who would only ever wring the dish rag extra tightly and mutter words under her breath about my recklessness. She'd usually at least get me Band-Aids, though. I never minded the smell of Band-Aids anyway. My mother probably did. Or she never really thought they had much of a smell, though in my opinion it always hung in the air around me like a dark perfume.

My mother's dead now. My mother's dead because she wanted to be. And by that I don't mean to say she literally killed herself. She wasn't generous enough to herself to do a thing like that. My mother would not pay herself a moment of intimacy with darkness; she stood only on the cold outer ring of it, looking in as an observer.

I instead mean to say that she woke up on Sunday morning, set the table with our large blue plates as usual, looked me in the forehead and said to me with dry eyes, "This is no good." And by Monday morning 6:30 AM sharp, I heard a small yelp coming from the kitchen and seconds later ran over to find her lying lifeless on the floor without a mark of agony on her soft pale face.

With as much simplicity and plainness as one saying they disliked dogs and then selling theirs the next day, so she disposed of her life, because she was quite done with it. The doctors said her heart attack was an utterly random tragedy, but I still don't buy that one. They don't know my mother, and how her mind could control anything, even her body.

I didn't attend my mother's funeral.

In terms of her life, there's not much to be said about my mother, except for the fact that she was a small woman who ruled the world of everyone she could fit herself into. Which was a lot, because she really was very small. She was seldom explicit in what she wanted, but she always got it. Most of her hours were spent pleasantly receiving the reverence she never raised a finger for but always lathered and bathed her whole body in.

I read in the newspaper that some coworkers at the small school where she taught described my mother as "active" and "motivated." She was commonly mistaken for those things, but in reality my mother never touched a thing. She voiced what was wrong with a situation, perhaps to no one at all, and waited for it to become changed. She learned to expect. Her life was perhaps the only missing link in that recurring pattern. Her life and marriage were the only things that never happened no matter how long she waited for them, and so she decided the whole thing was foiled.

My father was a high school science teacher, who yearned to be a physicist, who really was just an insomniac. He loved his work. He didn't study at any institution, but he read books of Newton and Schrodinger like they were pieces of the bible, and he was always in the process of writing something of his own and then crumpling it up and throwing it away because it was either "too much like Newton" or "not enough like Newton." He only wrote with his hands, never on a computer, because he was worried that the electronic space would rob invention of its wholesomeness.

He fell in love with his work more than he could ever fall in love with my mother. But that was mainly because nobody could ever fall in love with my mother. Love is only nurtured by pain. And she felt no pain. I believe she was the most miserable person I've ever known, but she felt no pain. A constant, quiet, droning misery. But no pain.

Pain is a wonderful, magnificent thing that I never got to taste too much of myself. I've only witnessed it in my father, in whom it always burned exquisitely. I never ceased to envy and admire him for this. I would watch him in fascination as he crumbled to his desk over his constantly failed work: his failed ideas, his failed paracosm that only existed during insomnia. It was drilling him to the ground, his stupid, stupid work that he loved so much. He went absolutely mad for it, and he was no good at it at all. He submitted twenty-five manuscripts to agents and editors, all of which were rejected and considered by his peers in the scientific community to be unfounded and radical. Once he wrote an essay defending Heliocentrism, and he was sure it would be the next *The System of the World*. But, of course, nobody was buying that load of bullshit, even when he later meekly claimed it was meant as an ironical work, and he had to throw it out eventually too, only allowing himself to weep over it late at night when he thought I was asleep.

He was never born to be a thinker in the ways he wanted to be. And he was never born to be an insomniac, because it's stupid to think anybody is born to be an insomniac. But he worked constantly to massage and nurture his thoughts. He probably never could do a decent job in his life because he never turned a full set of eyes outside of himself. Yet it was still his work and it provided him the most sacred bouts of pain that most of us only get to experience sparingly.

Besides pain, my father carried other things with him that I can remember. A smell of sweet honey whiskey always on all of his clothes and belongings. Even when he wasn't drinking, it clung to him like bees to real honey. Most people complained about the smell on his breath. My mother would overtly cough and cover her nose with her palm. But I loved the sharpness of it that lingered whenever he spoke. I loved him when he was drunk, and I loved him when he was crazy.

But he never noticed that I loved him at all, and so I adored him for that too.

Only a few months ago, my father told me about his last grand theory. I was the only one he told. We were sitting in the dark dewy light of his basement office when he said:

"You won't be able to understand this fully yet, but it's going to be over for us all very soon now. The ocean is heating up at a rapidly accelerating rate to the point where in less than half a year it will be hotter than the air temperature. Once that happens the Earth will be heating from above and below like a grand convection oven and destroying all life rapidly until we end all together. We'll all be reduced to nothing."

He showed me his calculations, and I couldn't make any sense of them. But he was gripping my wrist and looking me fiercely in the eyes. And he believed so strongly in it, that much I could understand.

I didn't believe it much at first, but as the weeks went on and my father retreated more and more into his own mental space, spending days at a time in the basement, only coming upstairs for cans of Pepsi, it demanded my attention.

Finally, a week ago, for the first time since I was a little girl, I walked down the steps into the basement and called to him from his work. He spun around with his fingers pressed against his temples.

"What?"

"Dad," I said, my voice shaking. "What's wrong with you?"

"I can't do this anymore," he said.

I reached out almost instinctively to touch his face.

"Do what, dad?"

"I can't be the carrier of this information any longer." His voice was hoarse.

And I always believed his pain was beautiful, with the exception of the moment I saw it killing him.

"Let me do it, then."

"You can't be serious, my daughter." *My daughter* was what he said, something he used to call me when I was a little girl.

I nodded.

"Where do you want me to take it?" I asked.

"Anywhere that you can find someone who will listen."

And his whole body regained a curious amount of vitality as he sat up straighter in his chair and pulled folders from the shelves above him.

"The plan is to prevent this theory from dying," he said, flipping through pages of notes. "Above all else, the theory lives."

"Why does that matter if it's all ending anyway?"

He paused in his movement to look at me sternly then.

"Most simply put, it's to ensure we don't go down as the most pitiful species to ever exist. We can't be the ones who didn't see it coming. If there is life on another planet or dimension, any possible history of human beings that they may discover must uphold the most basic amount of dignity. I'll settle with being remembered as anything but naïve".

I understood, mostly.

"I believe you," I said.

He patted my head, and I felt my cheeks turn warm as the blood rushed to them.

I walked down the steps to the basement for the second time only twenty-four hours later to ask my father for further directions on my mission. This time, he was facing toward me, pointing a shotgun into his open mouth. I screamed and leapt forward as the shot rang out and sent his entire workspace shaking.

For three days I laid in agony beside him on the floor of the basement, weeping into his blood-stained jacket and shaking his lifeless shoulders. It was only on the fourth day, when I caught glimpse of a loose piece of his notebook that had drifted onto the ground, that I realized I had unfinished work to do.

I pulled myself up off of his body on the ground, which I had, until then, believed I was glued to. When I approached his desk and saw the scattered matches and piles of crisp black ash where notebooks and folders had once been, I punched the wall before me and cried out in fury, believing he had destroyed everything that I had left to live for.

Three more days, I sat still, watching his heap of a body. I sprinkled the ashes of paper on top of him like a showering of rose petals, despite my anger from the days before. When I went to pick up the last pieces of burnt notebook paper, I noticed that one notebook alone, tucked partway behind his desk, hadn't been incinerated. I held it in my hands like a piece of gold, turning on his lamp to examine the insides.

I scoured every inch of the book, only to find writing on the last very page. *Homeless* was all it read, scribbled out across the page and underlined in black ink. But then, when I flipped over the page and reached the back cover, something heavy was taped to the inside along with two index cards. The first one read:

My daughter, let me explain. You stop when one person believes you.

In black ink, taped on top of a shiny gray sixty-two millimeter bullet. And on the another index card taped just below the bullet was the bolded word: *YOURS.*

At first I felt sick to my stomach, and even dry-heaved a little on my knees there. But pretty soon I cleared my throat and pulled myself together. I paced around the room pondering it. How could I do this exactly how he wanted? What do the homeless have to do with this? Finally, I remembered something he had told me about his method long ago, when he was just beginning his studies as a physicist.

"Black ink," he had said. "I always use it sparingly. Blue ink is for the questions and the planning. Red ink is for the corrections. Black ink is the mission".

Entry Two

First I was very careful, and I watched them closely from a sloping sand dune east of their camp. It was my father's mission to send me here, I believe, because it's where the rawest people on earth live. In theory they're less prone to reject. They need to believe me; all they need to do is believe me. And so first I need to believe them. I took note of the fifty-seven tents; of the wood fire that burned and smoked every night of the week; of the little glass jar of money that was perched on one of ledges above the picnic tables and was never touched.

They sit at a set of three tables for meal times, and they typically eat out of paper and plastic bags. They eat things like sandwich crusts and apple cores and a lot of other types of dried-out bread things.

They seem to be rocked to sleep by the sound of the rolling waves every night in their camp. Once I watched a man run wildly to the water only to stop short at the edge and lay down softly beside it. The next morning, he walked back up the beach, caked with pebbles and sand, and he was greeted with casualness.

I stayed there for forty-eight hours on the slope, and not a single one of them noticed me because they never stepped over the strange asymptote that was the bushes in front of the dunes. They only ever went forward, to the ocean, or back to their camp. They never went to the side, and so I made it my throne for a little while.

I took note that about half were older folks, sixty-five on I would say, and they all smoked cigarettes that were thrown into the fire by evening. I didn't notice any kids or teenagers. Good, I thought, room for me and what I carried.

But a kid did notice me.

The first time I met Dragonfly was just about one hundred yards from where I live with him now. I was perched on my sloping sand dune. He took me by surprise; his entire existence took me by surprise, and I immediately distrusted him. He came up behind me, then carefully sat cross-legged beside me in the sand. His presence was so jarring, so extremely abrasive, that I felt myself pull back instantly. Why hadn't I noticed him before? Why wasn't he in my notebook? Why were his eyes so huge?

I needed to classify him.

Dragonfly. I wrote in my notebook. I traced the letters again. Made them real dark. Underlined them.

He looked over my shoulder.

"What are you writing?" he wanted to know.

I glanced down at him, because he was very small, and suddenly noticed that he was missing both of his arms. How had he slipped that past me too?

Has No Arms, I scribbled angrily next to his name in my notebook.

He read my notes again and scrutinized my face.

"I can read that," he said to me slowly.

"Well," I said curtly. "I hope you're okay with that name."

He considered it. "Yeah, it's fine."

I looked into his eyes then. I'll always remember my first time with Dragonfly's huge bug eyes, because of how they violated me.

"Stop that," I commanded.

He smiled incredulously. "Stop what?"

"Stop pitying me." Nobody had ever pitied me. It felt like something pinching the back of my neck. I disliked it very much.

He went on and pitied me some more.

Then I had an idea. I told him about the End. He could be my one person.

"The world is going to end. I don't have access to all the information about it, but I know it's real and we can't go down as the naïve ones".

And I regretted it. No, no, no. I have to be careful about these things. I can't let it pour out of me like this, I have to let it trickle inside of them. And oh, no, no, no, I did it all wrong already. Let me have another chance, Dad.

Dragonfly just stared at me for a long time until suddenly he sprung to his feet.

"Come on," he said.

I grabbed my notebook in a hurry and asked where we were going.

"You don't have anywhere to go but here," was all he said in response. And he led me down the slope and around the corner to his home in the homeless city.

"I'm not homeless," I called after to the stupid boy. But something about him had a leash around my neck. And I was following him anyway. The stupid, stupid boy.

"Yes you are," he corrected me as he showed me to my corner of the tent, where I live now, with the rusted lantern hanging from the ceiling and the pine needle-filled wool blankets spread out on the floor. And Dragonfly was a lot of things, but just then, for the first time of many, Dragonfly was right.

It was my choice to become homeless. Of course it was. I remind myself of this in late hours of the night when everybody is tucked away sleeping. It was, however, just as much his choice as it was mine.

Entry Three

A conversation I had with Dragonfly earlier today, the second day after my arrival:

You need to believe me, I was telling him, you just need to believe me.

And what do you need? is what he asks me.

I'm taken aback. This isn't about *me*, I gasp at him. It's not about *me*.

And he laughs at me. Laughs and laughs and laughs.

"Of course it's about you. Selfless, selfish. Same thing. Both all about you." And he laughs some more.

He is my biggest fear, my greatest enemy, the biggest threat to my method.

He'll never be the one to believe me. He's no use. I want nothing to do with him.

And I can never be without him. Nobody has ever told me I'm both selfish and selfless in the same breath.

He is the only thing I can think about sometimes.

I bite the skin beneath my nails all through the night, trying desperately to remember what it feels like to be completely alone again.

Entry Four

What is your name?
Taissa. My name is Taissa. And that's all I'll tell you.
How old are you?
It doesn't matter.
Where do you come from?
It doesn't matter.
Where is your family?
It doesn't matter. I told you it doesn't matter.
The people at the fire pit want to know about me, but it doesn't matter. They're already looking too far.
Ah, stupid bitch is no good. Won't answer any questions.
They leave me by the fire in peace.

Entry Five

Today I got into my first fight since being homeless.

Dragonfly had served me three crusts of bread at the picnic tables, and we were eating in silence. All of a sudden, a small memory crept into my mind of a woman climbing into our tent the night before. I spun around and tapped Dragonfly on his stumpy shoulder.

"Someone was in our tent last night."

He nodded.

"That's my mother."

"Your mother," I said.

"My mother," he said.

We ate some more. Dragonfly's eyes vibrated softly in their sockets.

"Sometimes she leaves. Then she comes back. She's got a wandering head, sometimes."

I nodded. Because my father had one of those wonderful things too. And I could remember her face. I could recall seeing the wiry strands of gray hair damply sticking to her face. I remembered gazing at her from within a sleepy confusion.

With moist eyes I had watched her mill about the tent, and she had looked soft; her movements lofty. The way she moved was something of a dream; she looked to me like an angel. Which was why I had promptly forgotten her up until this point. People who move like that slip in and out of your consciousness like handfuls of sand.

Dragonfly was rocking back and forth on the bench, his eyes cast downward.

I observed him with a careful curiosity and he immediately stopped his rocking.

Then, a man who I later learned identified as Sal slid on to the bench beside me and picked up a piece of my uneaten crust. He was tall and lanky with leathery tan skin and a marbled gray-black beard and eyes that darted around him.

Dragonfly coughed with obvious amusement and raised his eyes.

"Excuse me, but what the hell are you doing?" I wanted to know.

The man eyed me briefly under his outstretched arm.

"Eatin' my breakfast," he mumbled.

I looked to Dragonfly in angst. He only shook his head, throwing me to the wolves just a little bit. He had brought me here. And I believe he meant to feed me, and he meant to break me.

"You're dead meat anyway," I spat softly to the ground.

"What's that?" I had Sal's attention.

"You're dead meat, dead meat. Dead. Have your breakfast, but I have the knowledge. The world will end on you."

Sal spoke to me through a mouth crammed with wet food. Bits and pieces flew out of his teeth.

"You, my friend, are *wrong*." The table shook. "You know how many times I heard that same damn thing around here? Too many times."

He shook his finger knowingly at me. I should've known this wasn't the way to get someone to believe you.

"I believed the first ones, didn't I. Didn't I. Ah, I was an idiot back in those days. Not you though. You're just another one of those who come through here. You talk your nonsense. You're gonna leave soon anyway, aren't cha?"

I shook my head back and forth.

"No. No one else said what I'm saying. If you would just listen. *Just* listen to *me*. No one else has said it." I wished so helplessly that I had gotten to my father's notebooks before his matches had.

"Tell the girl to go away," he bellowed into the air.

"Tell the girl to go away," he shouted again. "Or I'll pull

a gun on you."

"You don't have a gun," I sneered at him.

"Where do you think all the other ones like you went? Huh? Think they evaporated? No, they didn't evaporate. Somebody had to get rid of them."

I pulled back, stood up.

"I have a gun too," I said slowly.

He eyed me, examining my face. He saw that I wasn't lying. Because I wasn't. I did have a gun and a bullet. But they were only for my suicide mission, and I could only use them once I knew I had made someone believe me.

Sal was obviously too stupid to know that I would never use it on him. He would waste his gun on me, probably.

Dragonfly must have watched all this wash over my face, because he was staring at me in fascination when I calmly took my seat again. Sal was muttering to himself and eyeing me with red-white eyeballs. But I was folding a napkin plainly over my lap.

"Do you want to eat my bread?" Dragonfly asked finally.

"No."

"That man's been looking for a war for years, Taissa. Don't be the one person who gives him what he wants."

Entry Six

And so there I was, at five o'clock in the morning, with the smell of Band-Aids again. I smelled Band-Aids inside one of the tents in the row down from ours. That pungent, pungent smell that I recognized so distinctively.

I sniffed the air.

Yes, definitely Band-Aids.

I wondered why in the world this homeless woman was keeping Band-Aids in her tent. But I didn't actually care. And then I moved on to the next one.

I was peeping my head in every tent this morning, getting a good look at all their faces. Wondering which one of them is going to be the one.

And something in it was actually sort of pretty. They're all little distorted snowflakes, and I didn't even bring my notebook as I meandered through the tents because I was enjoying it so much. And I inhaled deeply and savored the strange goodness in it all. And I was thinking to myself what a grand adventure it was to site-see to in the city of a thousand different freaks!

But then Dragonfly came up behind me, as he tends to.

And "What in fuck's name are you doing?" was what he suddenly wanted to know.

And "Looking, is all," I told him. "Looking is all I'm doing."

"Let the people sleep, you strange girl."

I thought I had lost him forever after that, I really did.

He hates me, he thinks I'm crazy.

But later that evening he approached me and asked me to come to campfire with him. He told me it would be worth my while to listen to some of the stories that the people have to share. But I wasn't really interested in hearing their stories, not tonight. I asked him to please go away, and he didn't argue.

Seconds before I had been terrified of losing him. Terrified, terrified, just to go on and make him leave without me.

I sat in a pool of cold sweat until he returned that night, and I didn't say a word to him when he unzipped the tent.

Entry Seven

"How did you lose your arms?"

And it wasn't that I'd been waiting to ask him that out of some form of politeness. I genuinely had not wondered about it until that very moment, as I was staring down at Dragonfly next to his mother in our tent. Because until then he didn't really seem lacking without his arms. But just then, I got the feeling that he wanted to hold his mother. He wasn't even touching her. He was sitting a few feet away from her, staring blankly at her sleeping body. But he wanted to hold her.

And I am so, so interested in him. I've never taken this much interest in somebody in my life. He's got these outward-turned eyes like I've never seen before. He never reacts in words to a psychotic episode of someone at the campfire or an angry outburst like Sal's, but if you watch him closely enough you can tell it's all absorbed through his flickering eyes. I want to freeze him where he is so I can take the time to just examine him. I can't freeze him, and he's always moving.

And I'm confused, because I'm supposed to be seeing the human being through a fine lens that has been tuned to pick up on the holes inside of their psyche. Holes for what I carry to squeeze in. I can see no holes in Dragonfly, so I keep telling myself to leave him alone. But there's no use; I could never leave Dragonfly alone.

There is no room for myself inside of him. And it troubles me, because I want to believe there's no place for him inside of me either.

There are no accidental holes in myself. Things travel through me only in an outward current. The End exhales through me. That's the only thing passing through my pores.

But then there his eyes are, when I tell him about The End. His knowing, mocking eyes. And I feel physically ill.

Nauseous. Why does he look at me like he sees right through everything I've turned myself into?

"I'm not telling you," he said softly.

I was struck. "Why not?"

"What makes you think I would tell you that?"

I was silent.

"Do you honestly believe you have a right to know that? Or you're just testing your luck?"

I fiddled with a blanket.

"Does she know?" I pointed to his mother.

And a sharp laugh erupted out of him. I winced lightly.

"She knows," he said finally, solemnly.

I stewed there in my own agitation for a few minutes, but the suddenly materialized concept of "the two of them" began to exclude me more and more as I sat.

Bitterly, I unzipped the tent and jogged forward out toward the water.

And it was a beautiful thing.

I could see the beauty in the water, I really could. I also could see why the people here tell stories around the fire. Things like that turn your soul inside out. I wanted to give myself to the water, just like the people here fearlessly give themselves to the fire every night. I can feel for the water, but it can't feel for me. And so things like that feel safe to donate yourself to.

I do feel for the ocean; the world, maybe. I love it even. But the difference is I'm not loyal to it. Do they understand? Do they understand that I'm not protecting the world or the people from The End? I'm protecting The End from the people.

Entry Eight

I came to the campfire, but only because Dragonfly told me that Sal was going to be telling a story.

When he stood up to face the circle of bodies around the flames, I made a point to glare at him with a burning intensity. But his eyes were flighty, and he didn't catch my gaze once. I angrily stared at him some more, but he still didn't make contact with me. Dragonfly sat beside me, smirking silently at my efforts.

"I'm gonna tell you the story of how I became homeless," Sal said. The people cheered a little bit. Some of them clapped.

"I was living in a big house in Hollywood before all this happened. Had two—no. *Three* kids. We owned a dog, even. A big Dalmatian named Daisy. I went to work real hard every day. Used to work at the Sheriff's department, and I was the head of all the officers. I told them what to do and everything, had a desk with my name propped up on it on one of those little desk signs. Anyway, one day, I's at work and a guy I know started shaking at his desk in the office next to me."

Shuffling in the crowd.

"So I go run over, ask my buddy 'What's wrong? What's wrong?' He doesn't answer me, course. Just keeps shaking and shaking, his mouth all foaming and everything. I don't know what to do, and I'm trying to call for help, but he's holding me down by the sleeve and asking me to stay with him. See, only a few others is working here because it's a national holiday and we're not even supposed to be in the office that day. But I'm still calling for help, and trying to hold him down. All of the sudden, he starts choking me. Arms around my neck and squeezing. And now I can't breathe, so I'm yanking him off me. And my arms around his neck now, choking him back.

And so the coffee lady walks in the office, screams when she sees me and calls 911. Of course I come out looking like the criminal, when I was just trying to save my buddy the whole time. You know what happens now, I lose my house and my job. I have to serve time in prison, and wind up out here 'cause I can't pay for any of that old life anymore."

Sal sat down, and people clapped.

"The end," they said.

I couldn't see Dragonfly's face in the dark, but I tried desperately to look at it with each flash of the fire.

Later that evening, I found Sal sitting on the sand.

"I liked your story," I told him.

He laughed. "Did you? So did I. It's a good one, isn't it?"

"Not really," I said. "It didn't actually make that much sense. I just told you that because I wanted to talk to you again."

He grunted. "Guess I'll have to take that into consideration when I think of the next one."

He reached for a lonely beer bottle sitting near him and poured a few drops into his mouth, then threw it across the sand.

"People leave this shit all over the sand," he mumbled. "Hardly ever anything left to drink in 'em. Worth a shot every time though."

I blinked at him.

"Sometimes, you get real lucky, and almost half the bottle is left. Out here wasters are our best friends, you know?" He cough-laughed and clasped his hands together over his belly. "What did you mean 'think of one'?" I asked him.
He coughed again. "Oh. I meant I would think up another story. You didn't really think that was a true one, did you?"

I was quiet. He craned his neck to get a look at my face. Then he erupted in raspy bursts of laughter. It sounded to me like he was drowning. I didn't care to save him.

When he finally quieted down, he told me: "The people here, kid, love stories. I've told a different story of how I've gotten homeless about five times here. They don't even remember."

Shit.

Shit.

This guy's a faker. They're all fakers. Dragonfly doesn't even know. Dragonfly thinks he knows.

"You think that's really how I became homeless? That really what you think?"

I grimaced.

He craned his neck again to look me square in the face.

"Who are you again?"

It occurred to me that he had no memory of our fight from earlier. His eyes were still the same red-white. But they weren't menacing. I decided not to remind him. "I just got here a few days ago," I told him.

He nodded, and there was a heaviness on his brow that took me by surprise. He looked old to me. But not old in its typical sense. Age in its rawest sense is not measured by how many years you've lived, but how many things you've lost. And Sal has nothing.

And I want to be around this man, who has nothing at all. He seems safer than Dragonfly. Purer.

"Do you know the boy with no arms?" I asked him suddenly.

"I know most people," said Sal. "Kid really likes you I think."

"He does?" and I believed him. He's a faker, a liar. But I believed him.

"Yup," he said. "He's a little bit fucked up too you know. His Mom's a little off her rocker. I think the kid needs you."

I was quiet. "We argue all the time," I told him finally. "He laughs at me."

"Kids like him need to argue. Spend too much time in their own heads."

"We're almost always in a fight, I think" I told him.

"Well good. Fight with him. Yell at him. Tell him he's a fucking idiot as much as you want. He needs that more than most people need a hug."

"Okay," I said.

He smiled a little bit, I think. I smiled a little too.

The ocean was a listless thing at the moment, becoming white noise all around us. It made my limbs feel heavy and natural on my body.

Then I remembered something I needed to tell him.

"The world is ending soon. I don't have all the information about it, but what you need to know is the world is ending soon."

He craned his neck in that way. Looked at my face for a very long time. And then narrowed his eyes.

And he remembered.

Entry Nine

This time at the fire it was a woman named Clara's turn to tell her story. She was probably about thirty but looked about seventy, and her vocal chords were already pretty much dead. Other than that, she was normal.

Normal.

Normal.

But then, at the last moment, a little bit to the left of normal, just like most things.

She stood up, looked at all the blank faces, and began:

"I have a funny story for you today, one that I can't help laughing through every time. Sometimes I don't even get the end out, but I'll see what I can do this time. Awhile back, when I was in my thirties, I had a beautiful daughter. She was oh, about seven. She was the loveliest girl you'd ever meet. But one thing about her was: she had to do everything on her own. From schoolwork to making meals to hair, she needed to do it all herself..." She broke into a snorted laugh.

The laugh sparked and faded in a heartbeat. It withered away, and I watched as her face went in motion from soft and feathery to coarse and callused. Her hands tensed and balled up at her sides. She shifted back and forth on her feet. She had been laughing just a few minutes ago. I already forgot what it sounded like.

Everybody waited. Nobody asked her to keep going. But nobody told her to sit down either. No boundaries, but no pressure. That's what you have here, is an abundance of space.

Inside this space, you can end up doing a variety of

things. Discovering yourself, becoming utterly and entirely free, and losing every aspect of your sane mind that ever fucking brushed your fingertips. Clara, standing in her universe of space, right there in front of the flickering fire and the white eyeballs, did a combination of all three.

The rocks at her sides flattened into hanging hands and fingers again, and she tilted her head back, and started to sing.

Ohhhhhhhhhhhh

I'm a Yankee Doodle
Dandee
Yankee Doodle Do or
Die
Die
Die

Dragonfly, on the opposite wood log from me, started to smile. I heard somebody clap his hands, and somebody rise to leave the fire pit. Shuffling in the leaves.

Shuffling.

Movement, soft movement.

Somebody started to say something.

But Clara cut in even louder

Ohhhhhh
She's a Yankee Doodle Sweetheart
Born Onnnnnn
The Fourth of
July
Lie
Lie

The shuffling stopped, and a few people started clapping their hands together. Clara balled up her fists again, and proceeded with her original story.

"I miss her, my girl. I can't even talk to you about how much I miss her. My daughter was my *light*. Do you understand what *light* means? Do you understand what light means? Do you understand what light means?"

She was parading around the fire, waving her hands back and forth all over the place.

She came over to where I was sitting and asked if I understood what light meant. I told her I always thought I had until right that moment. She didn't hear me.

When Clara was done asking people if they understood what light meant, everyone said "the end" and clapped for her.

Later on that night I saw her stumbling around the camp asking the benches if they knew what *light* meant. The benches didn't know.

Before we all went back to the tents, I whispered to Dragonfly. I told him my vault of knowledge. I told him Clara probably didn't even have a daughter. They all lied about their stories. Liars. Idiots. Sal's wasn't true either.

He told me I should probably stop trying to ruin things I didn't know how to understand. Clara might not have a daughter, he said. He also said she's not really a famous singer, but she thinks that she is whenever a group of people are watching her. It's pointless to call people liars, Dragonfly said, because even in delusion there is undeniable truth. Her words weren't the truth, maybe. But what we saw tonight was undoubtedly all of her.

I told him he was an idiot too.

And after all that, here I am again. Sitting in the tent writing in my notebook as the sky deepens and the maniacs enter their caves to rest. I'm listening to Dragonfly's breath harmonizing with his mother's. I wonder if anyone has ever told Dragonfly that he sounds kind of like an orchestra when he's asleep with his mother.

I wonder if anyone's ever told him that his sleeping breath fills the air that surrounds him almost enough to make up for the missing arms. Probably not, I decide. Probably no one has ever told him that.

I decide that tomorrow I'll describe to Dragonfly how his breathing sounds when he's asleep. It's the right thing to do.

How do you describe a breath, I wonder. I practice describing it to him in my head. I practice and picture Dragonfly looking at me with his huge eyes and understanding. It keeps me up for a little bit.

I end up back where I started, not really understanding how to describe a breath, yet understanding exactly how it sounds. Some things you just won't ever be able to describe.

You can't describe to someone who has never seen the ocean the essence of the ocean. But that's not because you can't feel its presence in every bone of your body when you give yourself to it. That's not because you don't really *get* what it is. The ocean is a different kind of soul that coevolves right alongside the human spirit in a certain type of way. We understand the ocean, and the ocean understands us. The relationship is unquestionable. The complex give and take of the water will always be comprehendible to us, more comprehendible than most things we pretend to understand.

But given a pen and paper, there is no way we could ever begin to put into our own words what the ocean is.

Right before I fall asleep, I decide that that's because the ocean is a different language than we speak, or will ever speak. We're not able to translate it into our own words, but it's supposed to be that way anyway. It's supposed to be a language we hear, but can't speak.

I don't speak the language of Dragonfly's sleep breath, not in the slightest. But I really do feel like I understand him when it circles the space around me like that. I really do feel the waves of his unconsciousness collapsing onto me. It's an intense experience as I lie in my blankets next to him. I'm almost afraid to move, so as not to shatter the little world that surrounds me. But at the same time, I'm also fearfully aware that there isn't really a way out.

I can't help but feel that I am so much more his when he isn't even conscious.

I didn't expect to be here.

I didn't expect to hear things in other people when they sleep.

I didn't expect to be here.

Entry Ten

I woke up this morning and took my seat next to Dragonfly around the sparkling embers in the fire pit. It was five a.m., which is when we usually sit here.

Dragonfly said he likes being alone out here. He wishes I didn't come out sometimes.

I said is it still being alone if someone knows where you are?

Dragonfly said why the fuck wouldn't it be.

I remembered that I have something important to tell him.

"Do you know what you sound like when you sleep, Dragonfly? Has anyone ever told you?"

"No."

"Well, you probably will never understand. Did you know that? It's just like trying to describe to someone the way the ocean is, or what a color is, or something like that. You just will never know."

"That's too bad," he said.

"Yeah, it really is too bad." Because it really is.

Then he told me that sometimes I acted like I was five years old, and other times I acted like I was over a hundred. I looked into the fire. The fire looked back at me. It saw me more than I saw it. I had to shield my face. Dragonfly watched me do this and assumed it was because of the heat. "Walk?" he offered.

Dragonfly had assumed wrong, but we stood up and started off across the sand anyway. We walked along the shore for a while in silence. Dragonfly is comfortable in silence. He listens to it more carefully than voices, I think.

He broke the silence soon though, because silence is only good given the assurance that it can be broken.

"Have you ever jumped off a cliff?" he asked. And he lowered his eyes, accidentally letting me in on a little bubble of excitement inside of him.

But then I glanced over at his eyes again, his huge bug eyes; how quickly and sharply they could buzz around his face. How they drew things all over him.

And I had to believe that nothing about him is accidental.

That's a similarity between us, is we're both completely intentional with who we are. The difference is, Dragonfly rewrites himself every day. I'm loyal to the being I once created at the beginning of all this. Dragonfly is loyal to no one. To no self. He takes a new form in every changing moment, and he loves every shape equally, yet mourns none of them.

And I think to myself sometimes, he's done it. He's figured it out. But I can't allow myself endless births. Loyalty leaves no room for love. If you are unwaveringly loyal to the self you make, it becomes impossible to ever really love it. But it's a commitment you make anyway, if you're the kind of person I am.

Had I ever jumped off a cliff. Dragonfly was the kind of person who would ask shit like that.

"No," I told him. Because I really hadn't ever jumped off a cliff.

"I haven't either," he said slowly. I felt the excitement travel through layers of the silence.

I knew where he was going with this, but I pretended I didn't.

He sort of knew it.

He nodded toward a cliff towering above the ocean. All up the sides were the etchings of erosion. The jagged cliff had talons and shrubs marbled all over it. The base sprouted from the ocean, from which the cliff spiraled all the way up to a peak. The very tip of it seemed calm and quiet. A different world up there, even from the parts just below it.

"That is a nice cliff over there, isn't it?"

"Yeah, it's pretty," I said. I scratched my neck violently and awkwardly turned my nose to the ground.

"Do you want to jump off of it now, or tomorrow?" he asked me.

I frowned and scratched my neck some more. Until that moment, the little jagged edges of the cliffs were just attachments to a big bell curve in the distance. But then suddenly, they were each their own little landing; each one higher than the next.

Each one very, very high. I wrung my hands.

"How do you expect to swim with your stumps?" I pointed out.

"I can use my legs. I've done that long enough."

I squinted. Because he really couldn't, that's why.

Dragonfly looked at the cliff and then back at me, then back at the cliff, then back at me. A mischievous grin was lifting his eyes higher on his face.

"What do you propose we do instead? Go home?"

Forty-two minutes later, I found myself staring down at the blue abyss. The wind blows colder when you're standing on cliffs, and it feels like it'll cut right through you or push you off the edge. You understand your own safety as nothing more secure than the apathy of the universe toward your being. This is what you feel when you turn your head upward.

However, looking downward forces you to consider the universe's accountability for your assured danger. Because although you are no different from anyone else in the eyes of the universe, upon this same logic can you conclude that the laws of gravity and kinetics will not spare you one bit.

Climbing up had been a struggle for Dragonfly, but he had found footholds and was able to slither his midsection up against the side of the rocky surface.

His chest and stumps were all bloody now. He was the

happiest I'd ever seen him.

I looked down at the endless blue. Blue, for ever and ever and ever.

Blue until your eyes hurt. Blue staring back at you, knowing you like the fire does. Blue that fucking scared you to pieces. But blue so endless that all of the sudden, you wanted to be inside of it.

Up there I had the thought that blue didn't really seem like the ocean. I told you about understanding the ocean, how we feel it inside of us. But blue is a different entity entirely.

I wanted to jump. I wanted to jump, mainly because Dragonfly wanted to, and wanting to jump off cliffs is probably contagious.

I stepped up to the very edge of the rock, and looked at the blue one last time. I was going to compare the way it felt to look at it to the way it felt to be inside of it.

I flung myself off the edge. I didn't do the thing that they always tell you to do; the thing where you make your body a straight little pencil so it doesn't hurt when you land.

I wasn't a little pencil.

I was like a big crazy blob.

Then the water hits.

The water hit me and I wondered if it was cement. Was the endless blue just a hard surface of cement painted in a color called endless blue?

It tricked me. Dragonfly tricked me. Everybody was lying, and I was probably dead. I would have guaranteed I was dead, laying face first on the cement colored endless blue.

Burning, burning in my lungs. I needed something. Oh, it was oxygen. And it was right above my head. I gasped for it. I heaved it in me, and felt the creases on my forehead soften. I shoveled more oxygen in like it was an opiate, admittedly feeling a little bit guilty of hedonism for doing so.

More oxygen in, more carbon dioxide out.

Arms making little circles at my sides. I was apparently not dead. I was very much alive, and cold, and instinctively paddling with my feet to stay afloat.

Then I realized that Dragonfly still hadn't jumped yet. I looked up and saw his bony body as a little extension of the cliff above. I blinked, and he was separated from it. A part of the air now.

If you've never seen a boy with no arms jump off a towering cliff into the ocean, you haven't seen much at all. He landed right next to me with a huge splash. I laughed at the incongruence between his body and his splash. Then he started kicking wildly, his head bobbing just above the surface. He was swimming, sort of.

We found a buoy close to us, and we rested. Dragonfly inched his torso up onto the widest part of the buoy, and I held onto the side.

I watched the evolution of his face. Inside him, colors spilled. Colors changed. Inside him, everything was new.

The blue had turned him into a repository of textures and colors.

"Tell me Taissa!" he shouted. "Were you scared? Or did you love it? Or maybe-- maybe were you scared of loving it?"

"It wasn't very bad," I told him. But I feared that he knew that inside me, the colors were spilling too. I felt them leaking through my veins.

"But why did you take so long to jump?" I wanted to know.

"I wanted to make sure you were watching." He smiled at me.

I reached out and touched his cheek suddenly, recalling the euphoric feeling of resurfacing after being plunged into the water.

"I don't think I want to die," I confessed at once, my lips trembling.

I feared he would mock me like he knows so well how to do, but the muscles in his face were unmoving, serious.

"Of course you don't," he said. "That's why I took you jumping. At the brink of death, life is exquisitely rich."

We sat there again, basking in the silence. We bathed in

the silence until our heads stopped vibrating. We floated there until the water was cold again.

It stopped being a pool of blue, and turned back into just the ocean, the same ocean we understood so well but aren't capable of explaining.

"We should start swimming back," Dragonfly said abruptly.

I almost argued with him, but I didn't because I remembered just in time that the kind of person I am wouldn't argue with him about heading back.

We started back toward the shore. I kicked my feet around and tried to swim the way Dragonfly was. Just to see.

It tires you out fast, though. He was getting tired out, too. I saw it in his face. The colors were leaking out of him, but not in that watercolor way. They were leaving him completely. He was just a pale, pasty shade of helpless.

About a quarter mile away from shore, Dragonfly started doing this thing with his head where he'd crane his neck really far up and gasp for air, then sink it just below the surface for awhile, all the while splashing his feet all over the place. It was getting annoying, really. Then I realized that he was actually kind of drowning. Dragonfly would never admit to that, though. Dragonfly's the kind of person who would never admit to drowning.

Pretty annoyed at this point, I said to him, "Dragonfly, can you please not drown a quarter mile away from shore?"

He scrunched up his nose with determination. "I'm not drowning," he said between breaths.

We made a little more distance back, and his breathing was getting more and more choppy. His head fell under for a bit too long, then. I pulled his head up out of the water and tapped him on the shoulder.

"Yes, you are drowning, Dragonfly."

"No, I'm not," he gasped angrily.

"Actually, yes you are."

He just glared at me then, flailing around a little bit and struggling to keep his head above water. I smiled at the thought of being right.

He was kind of drowning right in front of my face, though, so I sighed very heavily and then lifted his torso above the water in front of me.

He pretended to resist it, but gripped his ankles together tightly around me and clung on.

We didn't say anything for the swim back. It wasn't a very pleasant silence, though.

I fell into a rhythm of carrying him and I believe he enjoyed himself despite how unentertaining it was for me.

Upon reaching the white sand, I threw his body down onto the surface and lay beside him.

We both lay there for some time, breathing heavily. When we caught our breath, we stood up and started walking across the sand.

He was mad at me, I could feel it.

"You're not that great of a swimmer," he muttered.

I snorted. "You should teach me then."

He kicked some sand. He knew I was right. I had been right a lot of times that day.

"You didn't have to *save* me. Why did you do that?" he demanded.

And I knew I didn't have to. I told myself I only did it to keep him alive until he believed me.

"I have my reasons," I muttered.

Entry Eleven

Dragonfly's mom was stirring when I woke this morning. It was just the two of us in the tent, and the fabric walls felt smaller.

A repetitive scratching noise was reverberating from some side of the tent, and I finally had to sit up to see where it was coming from.

Dragonfly's mom was sitting hunched over in the corner of the tent with her back to me, her elbows moving back and forth.

I silently crawled over to her side and peered over her shoulder.

In her right hand was a piece of rotten banana, and in her left was a chunk of charcoal.

I squinted my eyes to see that she was producing something on the inside wall of the tent.

She must have felt my breath intrude her space, because she whipped her head around to face me.

I lurched my head back at the confrontation of her eyes. They were like Dragonfly's, except for different. They were wide and huge like his, but overcast with a sort of grayish film that crept from the corners into the pupils.

My jolt of fear made her laugh, and her shoulders shook. Then she remembered what was in her hands. She pointed to the inside of the tent facing her.

"I'm just drawing here!" she said cheerfully to me, and

picked up her charcoal again. Her hand pulsed back and forth urgently and the scratching noise set in again. Then she jabbed the banana into the tent three times, and repeated the process.

"Just drawing!" she said again.

I widened my eyes and crept backward. Just before I unzipped myself out of the tent, I peeked back one last time to see her body vibrating in the corner like a little machine.

I shook my head and sat by the twinkling dust of a fire with Dragonfly.

"Do you want to jump off another cliff today?" was the first thing he said to me.

"I don't want to drag you back to shore again."

"I'm not serious," he said, "I just wanted to see what you would say."

We sat in silence for awhile, but it was silence with rounded edges.

Lots and lots of space. Space, like Clara had that day.

Space to do anything.

I pulled out a pad of paper and began to write, obnoxiously raising my elbows to shield my work from his eyesight.

I scribbled away for a while until I felt Dragonfly's neck shadowing my page closer and closer.

I glanced up at him, then back down to my writing.

"What are you writing? Is it the same thing you write in that notebook all the time?"

"No," I put down my pen for a second. "It's not the same thing I write in my notebook. I'm rewriting a story."

"What story?" He was getting curious. Dragonfly looks very small when he's curious and I had the thought that it made him seem very ugly.

"Snow White," I said finally.

"Why?"

I tapped my pencil impatiently on the pad of paper. "Because I rewrite things," I explained, "and this one needed it."

"Read it to me," he commanded. It was a pretty good

idea.

"Okay, so the original version of Snow White goes like this: Snow White is awoken from her sleeping death by the kiss of a prince and runs off with him and all that stuff. Right?"

I looked over at Dragonfly. He was tilting his head in shy confusion. It hadn't occurred to me until then that he's probably never seen Snow White.

I'd always assumed he was born like a normal kid and then moved to the homeless camp, but at that moment I began to wonder if maybe this is the only life he's ever known.

He was still waiting for me to finish telling him about the way Snow White goes.

"Well, you can entertain yourself by reading through fairytales at the library another time if you want, because I rewrote one and made it much better," I re-focused him.

"So, in my version, Snow White and the queen are actually the same person. They're just different versions of each other. It goes like this: the little princess lives purely in her own little world. The wicked queen lives in *her* own throne of evil, and is constantly trying to kill Snow White. One day, little Snow White decides she is too disgusted in the queen's evil to bear it any longer, so she stabs her in the chest while she's sleeping. The story goes on, and you'd think that everyone lives happily ever after now that the queen is dead. But one day, sweet angel Snow White looks in the mirror and sees the evil queen staring right back at her. Horrified with herself, she penetrates her own chest with the same knife, eventually killing both versions of herself, in her attempt to wash out each extreme."

I closed my notebook and looked at him expectantly.

"The end," I said.

"In the original version, they don't have 'the end'. It's called happily ever after," I explained to him.

His eyes grew wide. "So, there's no end, really, in the original version?"

He was still grasping the idea of a fairytale and I waited impatiently for him to catch up.

"I guess not," I said. "But happily ever after is still an ending, Dragonfly, it's just their version of one. Not that that's even the point of what I just read you."

"No it's not," he argued, "*Ever after* implies that it actually never ends, that it just goes on for as long as you want it to."

I tapped my fingers on my chin. "Mine is much better, don't you think?"

"It's good. Yeah. But can you tell me about the other one?"

"I knew you would like it," I said.

Dragonfly looked disappointed. He was probably wondering if he could actually go to the library and read about Snow White. He was probably wondering if I had just made up the whole entire idea of fairytales anyway. It was my turn to wonder about something, though.

"So, Dragonfly, are you going to tell me how you lost your arms or what?"

He looked down and dragged a pinecone across the ground with his foot.

But just as I thought he was about to speak, Sal and Clara kind of invited themselves to sit down next to us at the fire pit.

I shifted in my seat. I remembered the way Clara's face had changed forms at the bonfire the other night. It was stranger to see it in a state of steadiness. I decided that she didn't wear normalcy well and that it looked crazy on her.

"What are you two up to?" Sal slapped Dragonfly on the back before taking a seat.

"Taissa was reading me her new version of Snow White," Dragonfly explained.

"Oh," Clara said, "I wrote Snow White. That's how it became a film, is I wrote it and sent it to them."

Sal laughed loudly and Dragonfly cleared his throat.

"Well I just wrote a better one," I said to her.

And then we left.

It's dark now but I'm not sitting in the tent. I'm sitting on the shore of the beach, feeling the water trickle through the cracks of my toes. It feels nice, in the way that most things don't.

I spin my head and neck all around me. Not a soul in sight.

And here I am letting my elbows sink into the sand when I take a break from writing notes. I discovered just a few moments ago that when pretty much all you ever do is write notes, it's nice to let your elbows sink into the sand sometimes. But then you can go back to writing, and your elbows coil up again inside their little elbow cavities and it feels like they were never in the sand at all. You really can.

If I turn all the way around, there's this row of shorefront homes.

Blue.

Brown.

White.

Most of them an orangey-yellowy color.

All stacked up right along the edge of the cliff there.

Windows, walls, terra-cotta, stucco and burnt wood. Glass windows facing the shore. Glass windows facing each other.

They each have sea walls structured in front of them, and you can see the imprint from where the ocean tried to wash the walls away. The ocean tried, but all it really did was brush the walls smooth and silky to the touch.

I did touch one of the sea walls once.

They really are smooth and silky to the touch.

Once the row of houses ends, there's this gray cement wall that stretches just up to the top of the cliff all the way back to the start of the dry sand. All over the wall there's this display of graffiti in colors and shapes and symbols. People sprayed things like "Imagine" and "Fucked generation." Things like that.

There's this one corner that has "UNFINISHED BUISINESS" sprayed in huge boxed letters. One time I was standing in front of that corner, studying the letters, and I noticed the artist spelled business wrong.

Why would somebody ever be stupid enough to spell a word wrong in graffiti art, I asked Dragonfly later.

He didn't know why.

I ask Dragonfly about stuff like that sometimes, and he doesn't know why, sometimes.

But I still go up to that corner of the wall sometimes, and try to figure out if the misspelled word was purposeful or not. People on the beach eye me from a distance. They probably think I'm the one who spelled the word wrong. Sometimes I make sure they know it wasn't me, but they usually don't care to listen.

It's times like that in which I'm forced to understand the derangement of my own presence in the context of the rest of the world. Sometimes the clearest way to see your own reflection is right inside the whites of another person's eyes. And it's usually uglier than what you think you've been staring at in the mirror all this time.

But here, alone now, there are no reflections to haunt me. I understand the ocean in the best way; it doesn't understand me. And when you're around someone like Dragonfly all the time, you need a few moments where nobody really sees you that well. I bask in this here.

And I think I might fall asleep here. Right on the water's edge. The blue is drifting up further and further onto my legs, making me shiver and quake from the shoulders down. I wonder what would happen if the ocean picks up over night and drags me in with it altogether. I wonder if the ocean kind of wants me with it. Just to have someone's neck to wrap its fingers around. I laugh lazily into the small wave spilling over the sand and into my nest of hair. My conscious mind makes the slow transition into dream-like oblivion. It won't take me. It's bigger than I am and stronger than I am and crazier than anything I know, but I will still be able to fall asleep at its edge and not be overthrown by it.

Entry Twelve

I woke up this morning sputtering sand all over the place.

Sand is no good to eat, but even if you didn't mean to eat it at all you might end up with some of it down your esophagus if you fall asleep on the shoreline.

The muscles in my calves were all seized up, and my neck had a ball-like knot in it. The caps of my shoulders were being shoved into my jawline, and it took me awhile to realize I needed to readjust my body for this to change.

I slowly lifted myself up to my feet and brushed some sand off of me, smacking it carelessly off my arms and the backs of my thighs and my shoulder blades. But lots of it remained caked on all over and hidden throughout my body's crevices.

After that I dragged my feet up the sand, past the lined up houses, past the graffiti wall, past the misspelled "business," all the way back to the camp site. Dragonfly was waiting for me at the embers. His eyes scanned me up and down.

"Where've you been?" he asked.

"I feel bad," I announced and threw my body on top of a log.

Dragonfly nodded.

We were quiet for a little.

I lifted up the corner of my shirt and located the little spot of tar that had apparently clung to me overnight. I started to pick at it with my thumbnail.

Dragonfly watched me.

"That'll be the last time you'll do a solo beach night, I assume?"

His voice presented itself with such dispassion that I almost believed the question was nothing more than a meaningless formality.

Yet somehow, I didn't believe it.

I stayed concentrated on my shirt. I tried spitting on it. It didn't work.

"Shit," I said. "Tar really doesn't come off, does it?"

Dragonfly leaned in closer to me.

"So that'll be the last time you spend a night on your own?"

I shifted my eyes to the sparks, then to the stones on the ground.

"Do you think using water and soap would help?"

"Everybody does it within their first nights here," Dragonfly said. "Everybody tries that. I tried it my first night here."

Damn tar.

"Everyone gets tired of being in such a dirty, crazy, disgusting group of people. Everybody thinks it's a great idea to run off and spend a night alone. Right in the soft sand of the beach, or by the cliffs, or down by an ocean cave filled with seaweed. Right?"

Damn tar. I wonder if I took a rock... Damn tar.

"Everybody thinks they need some *normal* time for once. They're getting tired of all the crazy. Everybody tries to escape the crazy," He laughed.

I shivered, because his laugh was cold and short.

The tar still wouldn't come off.

"I know you think you're normal, you asshole," he spat. "But those times on your own, when you think you're running away, I should tell you that you're just closer to the craziest thing of all out here: your own mind."

He bit the sides of his lip and nodded slowly. His eyes were electric.

"Yep. Your own psyche. The one you think can pull you out of all this when shit gets too bad or help you escape the homeless camp here and spend nights on your own. Well I hate to be the first to tell you, but you lost your plan B a long time ago."

Tar. Shit, sticky sticky tar. Tar is so stubborn. Shit.

"How's that for normal? It's not," he spoke sharply and precisely, sounding out every vowel; spitting out every t and s. "You're not normal. Nobody is normal. *You are one of us too.* You bitch."

He was leaning down and seething this into my face.

My fingers were all sticky. All covered in goo. The corner of my shirt was smeared with black. I sunk my chin in my hands and let the black smear all over my lips and my nose and my eyelids. I stopped fighting the damn tar.

Dragonfly spit into the fire and rose, his body lengthening again.

He kicked a log as he walked in the opposite direction of the camp.

As he was leaving, he called "Peanut butter" over his shoulder.

I straightened up in my seat.

"What?" I yelled after him.

"Peanut butter's how you get it out, you bitch," I heard him yell just before he disappeared around the corner of the first dune.

At the campfire, Sal asked me where Dragonfly was. I told him how would I know? Was Dragonfly my dog or something? How would I know all of Dragonfly's whereabouts? It was stupid of him to ask me that.

Sal raised his eyebrows at me and said, "I assume you two aren't getting along."

"Dragonfly had a meltdown," I mumbled.

Sal nodded, but kept his eyebrows raised at me.

I narrowed my eyes. "He did. He's crazy. Really crazy. Just goes on and on about nothing. Doesn't know what the hell he's talking about."

Before everything got quiet at the campfire, Sal leaned in close to me and whispered, "You smell like peanut butter."

I tried to explain to him that I found some peanut butter in a tent and rubbed it all over my tar spots earlier today, but he just nodded at me and refused to lower his eyebrows. I muttered things to myself and gave up on trying to explain.

Another woman told a story tonight.

"My name is Amber," she said. "I'm blind," my eyes shot up to hers. They looked glassy. Glassy, but present. They made direct contact with mine, and I tilted my head to the side at her. I leaned over to ask Sal about it, just to see him laughing quietly and rolling his eyes in his seat. I sat back.

"All I want to do is see the world. Look into the clouds and see the pretty birds. Watch the trees swing back and forth. Watch little animals crawl across their land. It would be so lovely. But I can't see anything. It's all blackness to me. Nothing." She paced back and forth in front of the fire. "Here's how it happened. I was living in a mansion. I used to live in a mansion, you know. I did. With a puppy. And a dog. And some cats. And some birds. And some horses. And some" she drifted off. "And some. And some. One day I was walking outside to go to the supermarket, when I felt something hit me out of the sky, and I went blind right then and there. Right then and there. What it was, was God punishing me for something. Still haven't figured that out yet. For something. For something. Don't know what. But then, I was so blind I walked all the way to this beach camp. And I ended up here. I'm still so blind now today. Can't see nothing. Can't see a thing. Not a thing. God punished me. For something. For something."

"The end," the group said.

Sal was laughing and shaking his head.

"She's my favorite" he said. I squinted, because I still couldn't forget the way his eyes looked that day at the breakfast benches. And I couldn't understand where they went.

"Good entertainment tonight, huh kid," he said. I didn't answer. I was watching Clara gracefully find her way back to a log.

I waited until everybody had left the campfire.

I waited until the fire had almost completely subsided.

I waited until the sky was a creamy shade of midnight.

I waited until the sky was a creamy shade of lonely.

I waited until nothing looked alive anymore.

I waited, but Dragonfly didn't come.

My eyes were beginning to grow hazy. I slumped in my seat.

He was crazy, I thought. Just saying all that nonsense. All that nonsense. He's out of his mind.

Out of his mind. An Idiot.

I snorted to myself. He went on and on to me about all that nonsense. Too bad he's just crazy. Just a crazy, crazy idiot boy.

Crazy, idiot boy.

But then.

As the absence of Dragonfly filled the air almost as much as his presence, something came over me. And I opened my eyes a little bit. I lifted my head up. And I started to wonder. Dragonfly was just crazy. Just a crazy idiot boy going on and on. But what shook me right then, is I started to wonder if maybe that was his point.

Nobody can escape the crazy, he had said.

So I jumped out of my seat, and all the blood instantly traveled to my skull. I stumbled around a little, and then sprinted as fast as I could past the first dune, past the first stretch of sand, and out in front of the graffiti wall. This time, though, I wasn't really running away. I stared at the "UNFINISHESD BUISINESS" and kind of threw handfuls of sand at it.

Normally, I would've laughed to myself at the thought of what I looked like from an outsider's perspective. It wasn't long ago that there was a real formula to this whole mission.

But tonight I realized that at the start of your time out here you feel like you're stuck in this horrible misconception. The maniac that expresses itself through your own existence is a terrible misunderstanding that you never have the chance to explain. That's what it feels like.

Tonight, I understood that *this is exactly what it looks like.* I'm a person with sharp backbones and matted, sandy hair caked with peanut butter and tar, who stares at the letters on a graffiti wall every single day and wonders if they're misspelled on purpose. There is no context.

I sprinted to the shore line and threw my hands in the wet sand, squeezing it through the cracks of my fingers and boring my eyes into the soul of the blue.

I was hoping to understand it. But I think now, somehow, it's different now.

Once you understand your craziness like this, it's not really about what *you* see anymore. It's not about what *you* see in the ocean or the sky or the fire, because your own pupils are riddled with distortion. Instead reality bases itself more on what sees you.

And you start realizing that what sees you is the whole fucking world. The *whole fucking world* sees you.

I will tell you now that I believe I was wrong. I was wrong when I thought the ocean couldn't understand me the way I can understand it, and I was wrong in thinking I'm safe next to the ocean, or anywhere.

I have to go find Dragonfly.

I have to go find Dragonfly.

The tar is all sticky in my hair.

Or it maybe it's the peanut butter. I smell like mildew. I have to go find Dragonfly.

I did find Dragonfly, but only when I gave up looking for him. I found him inside the tent, sitting straight as a pin, his spine pushing the mesh back a little. Maybe the tent should've been the first place I looked, but I think of him as more likely to be in the unordinary than the ordinary.

His eyes were unblinking when I crawled next to him.

When I saw him sitting there like a little pin, I kicked some pebbles around and yelled at him a little.

"Dragonfly, where the fuck have you been?"

Unblinking.

"God, do you know how long I've been looking for you out here?"

Unblinking. "Yeah, I've been watching you from here."

I stuttered, and then fell silent.

"It's about time you thought to look in my tent, huh?" he said quietly with a small, simple smile.

I sighed heavily and threw myself onto a pile of blankets in the corner opposite to him. I purposely turned my eyes down into the coarse material of the blankets. I felt them scratch my nose.

Then I remembered the whole reason I was looking for him anyway. I sat up and propped my back up against the pillows.

"I came to tell you that I understand what you were saying now."

He decided it was a good time to finally respond to me.

"Good. Now you have to actually do the hard part," he said.

"What's that supposed to mean?" All that I had done by the ocean was so clearly the hard part.

Dragonfly smiled widely, and the shininess of his teeth struck me just then.

"Realizing you're in captivity is a wonderful thing to do, but it doesn't mean you've found an escape."

And then he rolled over and slept like a log.

Entry Thirteen

I woke up this morning to a bleak numbness enveloping my body.

Mild sensation dangled off of me and tingled dully on my skin, but my insides felt impervious to the touch of the world. The remaining sparks of feeling made me even more miserable than if I had felt nothing at all, because each time I felt a small sensation I was forced to mourn the loss of the larger ones, again and again and again.

The greatest understanding I felt today was by the water. But it wasn't the one I wanted to feel. I went to the water to believe that this place had spoiled me from the inside out. I wanted to cry into it and let it too mourn the loss of me and my feelings. But like I told you, the water sees me now. And it made me believe that there was nothing really to mourn because nothing fundamental had changed in me since the day of my arrival.

I took all that with a solemn acquiescence. But now, laying limp under a heap of blankets writing, I've forgotten if it even made any sense.

The rays of light are penetrating through the thin material of the tent, and I'm squinting my eyes at the intrusion. I can hear Clara singing loudly outside. She's screaming,

"I will walk alone

By the black muddy river

Sing me a song of my own
I will walk *alone*
By the black muddy river
Sing me a song of my own."
I scream a little to drown out the noise.
Dragonfly stirs.

"Why are you screaming?" he wants to know. He sounds angry.

"Clara's singing too loudly," I explain.

Finally Dragonfly gives up on smashing his ears into pillows and ducks nimbly out of the tent. I watch him from through the mesh of the tent walls.

Clara is standing on top of one of the tables, surrounded by three other homeless people. She's thanking them for being such a great audience. Blowing them kisses and stuff. She says that she wrote that one, a long time ago when she lived in Massachusetts. Then she calls to him.

"You! You! Thank you for coming to my show!"

Dragonfly turns back to look at me through the tent for a moment.

"You're welcome," he says. And he sits down and actually does enjoy her show a little bit.

And I bathed in numbness, in those mesh walls, listening to Clara sing all day. I lost the urge to scream to drown her out because I couldn't really hear her anyway. I bathed in numbness until my eyelids wanted to fall off. It was getting dark. I wanted my eyes to stay open. I wanted to stay awake all night.

But I knew I wouldn't do that. Because I don't feel like fighting the battle against my eyelids. When you fight pretty much everything, you kind of want your eyelids to be on your side.

Entry Fourteen

Today Dragonfly took me on a long walk. He told me he wanted to go somewhere new, because he's always at the homeless camp. Always at the tents.

I told him 'always' is sometimes good.

We went on the walk anyway, because Dragonfly makes up his mind more than he does anything else.

This time we didn't walk in the direction of the water and instead traveled away from the beach and into the streets.

We became engulfed in civilization in a way that I hadn't been in a long time. There weren't many people out walking on the road, and I had the sense that we were in an area that sees little human activity of significance. Yet something about it still felt so manicured in the way the world outside of the homeless camp does. The fact that nothing was happening was so perfectly *right* that it could only mean it was an area of assured civilization.

I understood myself then as a tiny disturbance to the appropriateness of it all and became amused. Every person within each vehicle that sped past us on the road probably craned their necks just a little bit to wonder at the two stick figures. I indulged these thoughts happily as we went along, something of a skip integrating its way into my walk.

I was lost in thought when I felt a drop of water bounce off my arm.

"Time to go back," I informed Dragonfly.

He was delighted, though, and didn't agree with the information.

I crossed my arms and bit my nails in obvious annoyance.

I secretly watched him with wonder.

He stuck out his tongue and ate the offerings from the sky. If he had arms they would be flailing all around like a little kid's.

I watched him carefully as he ran all around on the side of the road, his clothing slowly absorbing the pouring water and hanging off of him like wet rags.

When he glanced over at me from across the sidewalk in the pouring rain, I kind of smiled. Only because he wanted me to, though.

"This is perfect!" he shouted, "I knew something like this would happen if we just took a walk!"

He laughed and spun around. I followed him with my eyes. I held our backpacks in my arms, and I watched.

I watched until I got dizzy and tired. It was time for him to stop spinning. I wanted to tell him he should stop because I was dizzy and tired.

He ran over to me, panting like a dog, but not because he knew I wanted him to. "That was incredible!" He was spitting up water and shivering.

"Don't you want to go somewhere warm?" I asked.

"Let's walk more," he decided, looking somewhere up the road past me.

"More? But it's still raining." I looked up at the rumbling sky.

"I don't care," he said.

He didn't care.

And *he* loved dancing in the rain.

And *he* was glad we took this trip.

As we walked further down the road, I felt the numbness settling in again, comfortably this time.

You have probably heard otherwise, so I should tell

you that it is not beautiful to watch someone else dance.

Entry Fifteen

We got up and found breakfast out of dumpsters.

We had fallen asleep on the side of the road after Dragonfly had promptly decided he was too tired to walk anymore. I had inquired whether or not his mother would wonder about us, and Dragonfly had pretended not to care either way.

I had half of a brown banana.

Dragonfly had the crusts of a peanut butter sandwich.

The trip as a whole in its most basic sense transformed us from homeless to the disgusting kind of homeless.

Then we walked until we reached a buzzing part of town. There were restaurants and theaters and billboards and the constant hum of mid-morning conversation.

There was a billboard with a glowing woman's face.

It read: "The teeth whitening business that will put a smile on your face."

It didn't spell business wrong.

The glowy woman looked happy about that. We saw the kind of places with drink menus standing vertically on outside tables, and heating lamps (turned off because it was a warm morning), and fake daises in vases with little pebbles.

People with sunglasses, people without sunglasses, people carrying brief cases and people carrying babies.

Billboards, billboards, more billboards.

Words spelled right on all the billboards.

Glowy women with white teeth.

I was overwhelmed. I couldn't stop looking around. Dragonfly watched me impatiently.

"You act like you've never been to the city," he said.

"It's been awhile since anything has had this much life

in it," I told him. But he was already crossing the street.

I stumbled after him.

It never stopped. There wasn't any silence, not in this part of town.

Each time a street ended, a new one popped up with more noise and more laughter.

There's this way about the street corners that drags you around and unwinds you in slow motion.

The air was biting then, crisp, sharp, cold. The streets billowed with cigarette smoke and six-inch heels.

I was barefoot, and my feet were aching. Dragonfly was wearing shoes, though, so he was okay. We crossed more streets, passed through more corners, unraveled by the city air. And for moments I thought the numbness was thawing. For moments I thought I could feel the pain traveling from my heels all the way up my thighs.

Pins and needles.

Pins and needles.

Almost clear of numbness.

But no

Just perception

Not sensation. Hansen's disease: It's when you can't feel the sensation of pain. But the thing with that is, if you held your hand over a stove and weren't able to feel the incinerating heat, you would still get burnt to a crisp.

Burnt to a crisp, really.

I really don't have Hansen's disease, though. To think that would be stupid. But if I did I would get burnt to a crisp probably. I can't let it happen that way. I have to do this the way Dad wanted.

I was lost in thought when Dragonfly stopped me on the sidewalk.

The signs above us read "Tickets Here."

We were standing in front of a movie theater.

Well, Dragonfly was standing in front of a movie theater.

I was leaned up against the wall of it, my knees

knocking together and folding over.

"Sorry, it was a lot of walking," Dragonfly said mindlessly, glancing around. "I wanted to see a movie in a movie theater."

I blinked at him. "I think you have to be un-homeless for that."

"I have money though!" he grinned.

"You have money," I repeated. "We ate out of dumpsters today, and you have money."

He smiled in spite of himself. "I wanted to go to a movie. That's the reason I wanted to come to this part of town."

"I stole it out of the begging jar," Dragonfly explained to me.

I was starting to regain some of my balance. My knees were just beginning to feel okay.

"You stole it?" I tried pictured him propping the glass jar up with his feet and gnawing at the dollar bills with his front teeth. I just couldn't quite figure out how he did it.

Everybody puts their begging money in there. It's what they do.

But strangely enough nobody really ever talks about the begging jar or thinks of the begging jar as an escape or even looks at the begging jar. It exists there mostly as a decoration. It's selfish to steal from the begging jar, it really is. The begging jar has no real logistical significance, which is why stealing from it is that much more atrocious of a crime. In the same perverse sense that the two of us pierced the serenity of the empty street yesterday with our obnoxious existence, Dragonfly destructs the simple perfection in the nothingness by the mere act of touching it and making it something. Disturbing the almost divine slumber of a purely meaningless process so cruelly adds the disgusting value of the rest of the world to it.

But Dragonfly did it anyway, because he needed his own divinity.

Dragonfly told me he would go up to the ticket booth.

He would do the talking, and he would buy the tickets. He did ask me to pull the money out of his socks, which I promptly did and placed between his teeth.

I lingered back a little as he went, glancing nervously at the ticket booth. I heard Dragonfly ask for two tickets. I watched a man lean forward for a brief second, raising his eyebrows at Dragonfly. He awkwardly placed the tickets onto the counter and let Dragonfly decide how he wanted to retrieve them. Dragonfly decided he would slide them all the way to the edge of the counter with his chin and scoop them up in his mouth.

He gave them to me this way too, offering them to me from between his front teeth.

Because of my preoccupation with the flashy movie posters and popcorn machines all around us I didn't realize the movie he had picked until we entered our little hallway to the seats. *Snow White and the Seven Dwarves*, it read above me. I looked up at Dragonfly.

"I wanted to see the real version," he explained through muffled speech.

I scoffed in indignation. "It's just going make you realize that mine's better," I said.

"Maybe," he said, and his voice was heavy. But it was airy again within seconds. "I just want to see it. I figured it's something everyone should see. You know. Just to see it." he smiled a little bit at me, and I held my tongue.

Because I didn't buy it, exactly. I didn't believe Dragonfly picked out the movie just to have it under his belt.

I think he wanted to know what a fairytale is. I didn't tell him this, but as we waited for the movie to start, I wondered if he had done it all in the wrong order. It's supposed to go like this: First you see the fairytale and then you see the world. Dragonfly was going about it the other way around. People who try to go the other way around in the cycle probably go insane. It's just far too hard to be invited into fairytales and be able to keep one foot back.

Of course I couldn't tell him that.

Sometimes you have to let people do their own destruction in the same way that you would never touch an artist's hand while she paints a picture.

He didn't bring me there so I could save him from that, he brought me there so I could watch.

His tragedy needed a witness, his tragedy of becoming naïve, *the worst thing to be remembered as.*

Suddenly, I was quite sure of it.

The movie started.

Throughout the film, I periodically glanced over at him. He was glowing.

The way the woman on the billboard was glowing.
Mesmerized.

It looked so peaceful where he was. I had to keep myself from looking at the screen and at him. I had to close my eyes. Danger always looked so beautiful.

Finally I couldn't help myself. About half way into the movie I opened my eyes and watched him the whole rest of the time. I watched everything in his face until I knew it by heart. Every muscle, every twitch, every squint.

I watched it shift.

I watched my predictions come true.

I watched parts of his face move in ways that I had never seen before.

Edges on his jawline became softer.

I watched the transformation, and I let him go, doing all that I knew I was there for.

When the movie was over, Dragonfly spun his huge eyes around at me.

It made me squirm in my seat.

He noticed my discomfort and tightened up.

"You didn't have to look at me the whole time," he mumbled. I didn't realize until then that I had been holding my breath. I exhaled. My head felt lighter.

I shook my head and looked at him.

"That was great," he spoke slowly. "What a great movie."

"Was my version better?" I begged. "My version was better, wasn't it?"

He scanned my eyes. "Yes," he said, "*much* better."

After that, we walked back and crawled into our tent while all the maniacs were sound asleep. Dragonfly's breath crept and jumped in a softer way than I had ever heard it.

And I was pummeled with the sudden awareness of how *not home* I was. How far away from anything that contained me I truly was. All I could sense within me was a longing to be there. But not my house or anything. I ached to be at the *home*. I ached to be at The End already. I wanted to stop then. I really thought I did. The gravity of my own desire pressed me to sleep.

Entry Sixteen

I woke this morning and Dragonfly wasn't in the tent.

I wiggled my toes around beneath me.

I saw them move as little lumps beneath the patchwork blanket, but I couldn't really feel them.

I smiled.

In late hours of the night I'm terrified of my numbness, but in the morning I fall in love with it all over again.

I watched my toes curl, and I fell in love with the weight of lethargy on my sunken chest.

Outside of my little world in the tent, the fog had rolled over in the sky, and it was still sort of dark out. It looked dewy outside from what I could see.

I couldn't see anyone for awhile; all I could see was little dots churning around like melted butter outside.

Ah, melted butter.

My toes curling.

Everything was listless.

Everything was slow.

Until my eyes adjusted. The melted butter was gone, and I saw people; all the homeless people. Clear, distinct outlines of figures. Everyone was milling about frantically by the tables. Some people were yelling at each other.

My little island was jerked out from under me, and I was forced to snap my body up and into the surrounding world.

I found Sal sitting at one of the front picnic tables with his legs crossed and his eyes sunken forward. He was chewing deeply on a piece of beef jerky.

"What's going on?" I squatted next to him and pulled on his sleeve.

He ignored me. He was looking out toward the far end of the beach, the direction that none of us ever go. His eyes were zeroed in on something in the distance. I followed the trail of his gaze and kind of stared for awhile, occasionally glancing back at him, not really sure what I was looking at.

Finally, I saw it. I noticed it like a strike of lightning out of the deep grey.

Far off down the sand, standing next to the foaming water, a woman was thrashing around wildly. She was screaming, too, if you listened closely.

Then I ran.

Sal called after me with a mouthful of meat, telling me to wait a minute and to hold my horses but I didn't care about what he was saying.

I ran down the beach, my eyes fixating on the woman and reeling me closer and closer with each step. My lungs were aching and my knees begged me to stop pounding on them, but I still ran.

Finally, I reached her. I stumbled and bent over, panting all over the place. I pressed my hands on my thighs and looked up to see Dragonfly. He was thrusting his head back into the air and wailing. He was jumping up and down. He was running around her in circles. But for the life of him, armless Dragonfly couldn't do a single damn thing.

"Mom! Mom! Calm down! We've already been through this! Remember? Calm down! *Please!*" He was screeching.

"I can't believe you decided to do this now? Really? Again?" He kicked violently at the sand and it sprayed up into his face. "*I can't believe you're doing this to us again!*" he screamed, but I saw the wetness in his eyes.

Dragonfly's mom didn't hear him. She was thrashing around, kicking and spitting at the ground beneath her. Rubbing at her eyes; yanking at her hair.

Her left hand clutched her right wrist, wiggling it back

and forth.

"Why why why why?" she was muttering. Then, "*Why?*" in a screech.

"You always leave. Always leave. I had no idea where you were. *No* idea! I woke up one morning and you just why why why why…"

Something else possessed her body; something that maneuvered her every which way. The same thing that was crawling on top of the life inside her eyes the very first time I saw her, I figured. The same thing that operated her in the corner of the tent, mashing banana and charcoal on the wall. Dragonfly dropped to his knees in surrender.

"It's not my fault," he begged. "I didn't know you would freak out again like this, Ma. I didn't know. I was just gone for a little while." Tears dribbled down his upper lip.

Somehow the new softness that throbbed within his voice seeped through the chaos that she was so buried beneath.

Suddenly her mangled, clawing hands fell to her sides. Suddenly, she dropped to her knees.

I stood in shock, because seconds ago she couldn't have been soothed and quieted even by death. But somehow, when Dragonfly spoke helplessly to her it was liquid velvet. Somehow, it melted over her and massaged her from the inside out.

And she was tranquilized in an instant, still there on her knees with her head hanging like a docile dog. I watched in awe as Dragonfly picked himself up off the ground and approached her.

"It's okay, mom, I'm here now," he said. He was leaning over her crumpled body. I locked eyes with him for a moment, but he broke the contact quickly.

His voice caressed her deeper and deeper.

"I'm here, I'm sorry" he was whispering. There was no response from her, but instead she sunk down into a fetal position. She rocked back and forth and mumbled to herself quietly. She rocked, rocked, rocked. And repeated the process.

I stood in quiet amazement. I had never seen anything like it. I had never seen one human being pour heaven over another quite like that.

Dragonfly took a step back and stood next to me. We both watched her quietly.

"I shouldn't have left without telling her," he said finally.

I nodded.

"It's happened before," he said. "It's really not that big a deal. She just, you know, gets like this sometimes. When I leave."

I nodded.

He spat on the sand in front of us.

"Go ahead. You can say I-told-you-so. You can tell me we were wrong to go see Snow White in the first place. It was selfish".

I didn't look into his eyes. I was a little bit afraid of him after what I'd just seen. I stared at the bead of his saliva expanding in the sand.

"I told you so," I said. And it was selfish. But it was only as selfish as it should be. Dragonfly needed to go see Snow White. He spent most of his time being the feeder to a regression, and so for once in his life he needed to be the one to regress.

I walked back, then, back to the camp with Dragonfly by my side. I kept looking back at the big ball of his mother on the ground.

"It's okay," Dragonfly kept telling me. "She'll come back eventually."

But I wasn't worried she wouldn't come back. I was just looking at the shape of her, because she really did look so much like a big ball.

When I made it back to the tents, Sal was waiting for me expectantly.

"It was Mary, wasn't it?" he asked with a boyish grin.

It *was* Mary, I guess. I had only known her as Dragonfly's mom. But I liked it that way, and I kind of hated him for ruining it for me. He could just as easily ruin Dragonfly in the same way.

Suddenly everyone was crowding around me.

"Was it Mary?"

"The kid's mom?"

"He just left her, didn't he?"

"What an awful thing to do to a crazy woman. Just awful"

"Is she dead?"

"What was she saying?"

I pushed through the mass of bodies and stumbled over to the tent, gripping for the zipper. I looked back frantically to see them stomping after me in the pack of zombies that they are. I threw myself inside the tent and buried my head under the pile of blankets.

Numbness, again. Thank god, this time.

I must have fallen asleep for an hour or so, because my body jumped at the rustling movement when Dragonfly and his mother crawled inside.

She silently slid inside the tent and fell instantly to sleep. Dragonfly lay beside me and watched her with glazed eyes. She was sprawled out across the whole floor of the tiny space, leaving barely enough room for the two of us to squeeze together in one corner. I sat there then, listening closely to every breath that she took. It didn't take me long to realize that they weren't like before.

"Her breathing is very pretty," I told Dragonfly. I was lying, and it was a dangerous thing to do. But I sensed that he had asked for it.

He nodded. He let out a breath. And then he nodded again.

Dragonfly fell asleep soon after that. His head was resting against my shoulder. I thought, how nice it was that I could watch him even more closely like that. His face was baby-like and smooth up close.

I pressed my palms against his cheeks and I kept them there, because I had the feeling that he would be doing that with his own hands.

Then I had an itch on the back of my neck so I removed one hand to relieve it. But I kept the other there on the silky cheek where a hand belonged.

One hand for him.

Entry Seventeen

When I opened my eyes this morning, I realized that Dragonfly had already left the tent. His mother was still there sprawled out on the floor though. I stepped over her, unzipped, and found myself walking toward the fire pit. We'd missed a couple days of this part of our daily routine, and it felt kind of good to let my legs lead the way again. It was muscle memory, and when your body thinks, your mind just sloshes around in there.

I sat down next to Dragonfly. He was crying kind of. I couldn't think of anything to do about it.

He was crying.

All I could think of was that I shouldn't be there. And that I wanted it to stop, because he is noisier than usual when he cries. I like him when he's quiet.

"I can't save her," he whimpered.

"Don't be ridiculous," I said. "Of course you can save her. You can always save your parents. You just have to do what you should." My hands trembled. It was time to tell him about The End again; it had been too long. But the thought of passing it on to him was beginning to make me feel ill. I held my stomach in despair.

Dragonfly didn't notice. He was too busy crying.

Then something happened.

All of a sudden, a flicker of a reflective light pierced my eyeball. I jolted my head up and looked all around me.

A fluttering, zooming light.

Then again.

Then again.

It took me too long to realize it wasn't light; it was creatures.

Little, fluttering *dragonflies* circling us at the fire.

I turned. They were dancing over the whole camp.

Over the tents and the picnic tables and the bags of old food.

I nudged Dragonfly with my foot and pointed above us.

His red puffy, gigantic eyes questioned me.

"Look!" I said. *"Dragonflies!"*

Dragonfly looked around him at the emblems of his own being.

A knowing grin began to creep across his face.

"See? I told you. Dragonflies!"

But he wasn't looking at me anymore.

He was up off his feet, chasing a blue dragonfly around the camp.

There's this way about an armless boy relentlessly chasing something he could never catch, or even reach out and touch.

Something about seeing him gallop amongst the tiny embodiment of his own spirit made me remember why I named him that. And I wasn't angry at him anymore for being a liar.

I was the only one sitting by the fire then. He seemed to have forgotten I was ever next to him. But I didn't mind. Because there's this way about watching him that makes you not mind disappearing.

I took my seat next to Dragonfly at the fire that evening and I observed closely as he held an ear of corn between his knees and gnawed away at it with his teeth. He was eating neatly and precisely, without spilling a crumb. He had mastered the art of it.

Dragonfly turned his eyes toward me. They were lit with golden from the flames. His whole body was lit with golden.

"Have you never seen somebody eat?" he said.

"I have, but usually they have arms," I explained.

Dragonfly turned his back to me to finish his corn. I

kept peering around his shoulders to get a better view.

Then the story started, and Dragonfly was forced to turn back to the fire. I watched him in peace.

I planned on telling you about the story tonight, but I must admit I've forgotten it already. Or maybe I never really heard it to begin with, because all I could tell you is how Dragonfly ate his corn.

Entry Eighteen

This morning I didn't sit with Dragonfly at the embers. Instead I traveled over to the picnic table where Sal was picking at a piece of cinnamon-raisin bread. He kept smelling the little pieces, chewing them, then spitting them out into his palm.

"What's good, kid?" He said without turning around.

I straddled the bench next to him and pressed my fingernails into the wood.

He chewed intensely for a few minutes, then looked me square in the face.

"I'm gonna tell you straight up, you look no good."

I tried to sit up straighter and cover the holes in my shirt with my hands.

He took another bite and spit it.

"No," he said with a clump of bread under his tongue. "I'm talkin' about all that." He circled his finger around my face.

I spit into my hand and tried to violently rub off any dirt on my forehead.

He examined me.

"Mm no," he said. "It's nothing you can rub off."

I anxiously cupped my face in my hands and rubbed my temples.

"What do you mean? What do you mean? I always look this way." I shifted my feet under the bench. I felt a hotness in my belly, in my core.

"No," he said. "Not always. You've got something growing from the inside out. Put it this way. You ever seen the famous painting called "The Scream"? It's by a famous artist.

Jackson Monet I think."

I nodded.

"You kinda look like that. More and more each day now."

I pressed my yellow-brown fingernails into my forehead. "Well what am I supposed to do? If I can't rub it off? What am I supposed to do?"

I wasn't really asking him, but he genuinely considered the question for a good while. It wasn't until he had successfully chewed and spit out all of the bread that he turned to me again.

"I suggest you try holding onto the little things out here more than the big picture of who you are. It gets you by better."

I was puzzled and tired.

"What do you mean?"

"If you think of yourself like some big looming sickness that you carry with you, you'll never get out alive. What you need to do is each moment, become a different person depending on what's happening."

My head sunk in my hands. I didn't understand.

I was puzzled and tired.

Puzzled and tired.

No, no, no, none of it made sense.

"You're sick," he said. "We're all sick. But here's something for you to know. There is no such thing as a cure; it doesn't exist. But that doesn't mean you can never be well. It means you can only be well in little fragments of the day. You need to stop writing off little things because your sickness lives in the background. And most of all, get your shit together kid."

I shook my head in my hands.

No, no, no, it didn't make sense.

"You wouldn't want me to pull my gun on you, would ya?" His eyes flashed. And he laughed a long, toothy laugh. I remembered why I hated him that first day. If you hate someone when you first meet them and it slowly dissipates, you will always eventually come back to that fundamental aversion.

There is a cure: the cure is The End. He doesn't know it. But I do.

I was about to tell him that, but a voice in the distance jerked my chin from my clammy palms.

A man with a yellow-gray beard and beady eyes was standing on top of a picnic table, holding the money jar in one fist. The other was at his side, balled up. His head was tilted to one side. One eye bulged out farther than the other in his sockets.

I would rather look like The Scream than that, I thought.

"There's money missing from this jar. Somebody took some money from this jar" he was stating, so plainly and clearly that it sent a wave of eeriness over the place. Had he been screaming we would have been more at ease. But the way he spoke with words empty of conviction presented a much greater evil. I imagine the devil never screams. He speaks with bleak precision, exactly like this.

Faces emerged from tents. Hostile murmuring encompassed the people.

"I promise you, somebody stole. I counted a week ago and we had eighty-three dollars. Now there's only sixty-three," he said with psychopathic rationality.

In an instant he dropped the glass jar to the concrete. The impact of the jar hitting the ground set the crowd off, and we were mothered by chaos at once. Arms swung, ankles clashed, feet stomped.

And in the midst of the carnival, we each stood apart from the chaotic crowd, on opposite sides, with hazy eyes. I was motionless with my hands limp at my sides. He was vibrant, his hands nowhere at all. We stood witness to it all, yet mostly to each other.

"Was it worth it?" I asked him once back inside the tent.

"We got to see Snow White," he reminded me helplessly.

"You got to," I told him.

People outside were still raging over the jar they had never once used money from, though it had simmered down a little bit. I peeked out of the tent. All that was outside appeared to me as a brilliant performance. In every set of eyes outside there was an ounce of what lived in Dragonfly's mom's all the time. It was fascinating. I motioned to the chaos.

"Look what you've created."

His jaw twitched.

"You're quite the artist," I said.

"It was twenty dollars. Twenty dollars. How much could that have really done?"

I grinned a toothy grin. I pictured myself looking like The Scream.

It was a piece of art. I didn't mind it so much anyway.

"How much could it have done? I think a whole lot. I think it did a whole lot" I said with amusement.

"God damn it," he muttered, "I have to tell my mother."

"Dragonfly, no," And I was beginning to sweat. It wasn't fun anymore.

Sweaty, sweaty palms.

I picked a fingernail.

It came part of the way off. The other piece of it dangled painfully from my finger. A stripe of blood leaked out from under my broken nail. I pressed it to my lips.

"I have to," he insisted. "We made a deal. We told each other that we would always be honest."

"Times are kind of different now, don't you think? She's crazy now," I said.

Wrong. Wrong thing to say.

He narrowed his eyes in my direction.

"God, she's still my mother."

I wrung my hands.

Sweaty, sweaty hands.

"You don't even know where she is."

But that sounded to him like a challenge.

You say the wrong thing, you cover it with more wrong things.

"I need to do it now," Dragonfly looked at me, but not really at me. That's how I knew there was no point in saying anything else. Once I had lost his eyes, I had nothing else of him.

He ducked out of the tent, and I followed. We forced our bodies through the crowd of people.

Two bulldozers through a sea of zombies.

We bulldozed for a long while.

We found his mother sitting on the picnic bench, her knees to her chest, rocking back and forth. Her hands were pressed to her ears in so much focused tension that I couldn't help but find it amusing, much like watching a child in the middle of a rock concert.

Dragonfly must have seen this dancing across my face, because he angled his stumps away from me and spoke only to her.

"Mom?" I heard him say, as though he were knocking on the door and asking if she was home.

The inflections in his voice drew her out, as I anticipated they would.

She paused her rocking. "What baby?"

It was a funny thing, to see a woman in fetus position gazing up at a boy and calling him baby. But at the same time, Dragonfly too seemed small then. Dragonfly too seemed infantile as he stood in front of her with his bottom lip wedged between his teeth.

I needed some new entertainment.

I started to wonder what Sal was doing. Then I remembered that I hated him. I stayed to watch Dragonfly.

"I wanted to tell you something," Dragonfly said nervously. "I know we promised to each other that we'd always be honest, so I wanted to tell you something, because we promised."

She instinctively reached out her hand to feel him.

"Tell me something," she repeated. "You want to tell

me something."

"Ma, I stole money from the jar," he confessed. "It was me who stole."

"You stole," she said.

Dragonfly nodded. He closed his eyes. He waited in vain for her to actually hear him.

She sat in silence, her eyes drifting around for a while. He waited.

Something flickered across her face. She blinked, and cocked her head at him.

"You took the money from the jar. *You* took."

He nodded.

"I wanted to see a fairytale," he explained miserably, and I coughed in annoyance behind him, as if to tell his mother I didn't condone that stupid idea. "I just really needed to see the Disney version with the pretty girl and the singing animals and stuff."

But there was no point in explaining. The same terror that was once streaked across her forehead before we approached her was reconstructing itself, this time from the neck up.

The way she looked at him then, with the repulsion and horror as if he were holding a gun to her head, the way she curled her mouth up at the sides like a rabid dog took form with so much intensity and force that it almost sent me backwards.

Dragonfly painfully stood witness to what he had done to her and to himself.

He took a useless step towards her.

"Please, I didn't mean to," he begged.

"Get away from me," gurgled up from her throat. She extended one hand in front of her, and one over her eyes.

"Get away from me," even throatier.

He fell to his knees in front of her, hanging his head.

Beside him, I wanted to say I told you so.

Because I had. I knew the whole time because of my very own life. I knew that you have to be careful with things like that. That kind of love.

Anything with that much heaven oozing from it has the exact same dose of hell.

I'm writing in the tent now, and it seems that the whole world is asleep. It's a strange thing that when I'm talking to you in here, everything else around me seems extra nonexistent. The distant lights from the street seem darker, and the small noises around me are barely audible. If you're wondering about my numbness, it's still here. But the small sensations are slowly receding. For that I'm thankful, and I ease them onward in their disappearance. Only because I've forgotten what it feels like to love pain too. Now it seems to be such a burden.

Dragonfly still has his small sensations.

That's why things are more painful for him. Somebody should tell him to let go of freedom all together. Somebody should tell him things get a little bit easier that way. But they won't, and I won't. I wouldn't ruin the dazzling piece of artwork that pain produces; I wouldn't dare interfere.

Entry Nineteen

We went begging. We woke up early in the morning and huddled together. We were like a football team, except a little less team. And a little less football. So we weren't like a football team. More like a clump of bodies. We were in a huddle when Clara announced: "We're going to a different part of town today."

Muffled noises from the crowd. There was more confusion than there was anything else. Who did Clara think she was telling us where we were going? But the thing is, she could. Everybody followed her anyway.

"We're going to the pier," she said.

"No, we can't go there. I looked this morning. Cops are all around," I heard Sal say.

"I saw the cops too. It's good. It's fine," she told him. The yellow-bearded man seemed to be the only one who considered the idea.

"We do need to make more money," I heard him reason. "I assume you all haven't forgotten about the missing cash from the jar." Sounds of distress and anger erupted from the crowd.

And so we went. We grabbed our signs, and I gripped mine tightly as we walked. Dragonfly rolled his eyes when he read it.

We walked military-style across the dunes, through the beach parking lot, into the cross walk and onto the sidewalk.

We were a swarm of bees, and people responded to us in that manner, stepping out into the streets to avoid being brushed by our arms. I didn't mind that, because I didn't want to be brushed by their arms either.

The crowd didn't mind either. Each person only had one priority, and that was to keep close to the shoulders of the person two steps ahead. Clara, leading the pack, having no shoulders in front of her, must have been following something else.

We arrived and spread out old blankets and jars. Clara brought some jewelry to sell, and Amber even brought her triangle, because she plays the triangle. It usually draws in a crowd, mostly because it's an entertaining thing to watch a blind woman play the triangle. Nobody ever really gives her money, because she's kind of horrible at it. Usually they sheepishly slink away after awhile, believing that she never saw them standing there in the first place. But she does; she feels them there. She's told me that before. I once asked Amber if she knows she's horrible at playing the triangle. She told me she eventually figured it out that everybody else hates it, but she likes the way it sounds in her own ears.

I sat cross-legged on my blanket next to Dragonfly, holding my sign in front of my chest.

"All I need someone to listen to a very important theory"

Dragonfly kept side-glancing over at me and rolling his eyes at my sign.

"Nobody else wants to listen to stories told by the homeless," he said.

"It's not a story."

I thought about it furiously.

I thought about it so much that I almost didn't notice a mob of people swarming Clara's blanket. There were three officers crouched around her. One of them had black hair with a clipboard. None of them had faces that looked like anything. I sprang up and moved closer, then hesitated back as I heard Clara's shrieks.

"I just think this bracelet would look so good on you!" she yelled, gripping a young girl's wrist and forcing the beads onto it. The girl was crying and screeching all over. She tied desperately to yank her wrist away, but Clara's grip was strong.

The three officers were yanking her arms back and

releasing the girl.

The girl made a move to run away, but an officer stopped her for questioning.

"She tried to sing to me, then she tried to put the bracelet on me, then she wouldn't let me go!" She cried.

"Ma'am, we're going to ask you to leave. All the rest of the beggars as well," he spoke calmly.

"No," Clara said. "No, we will not leave. No you should not have taken that girl away fro me. The beads were her color. The beads were really her color. Really her—"

"Ma'am, we're going to ask you to leave one more time," the officer spoke a little louder then. He planted his feet right in front of her. His face still didn't look like anything. It appeared to me as just a mouth moving and twisting all about.

Clara set her bracelet down softly on the blanket and a sigh of relief so subtle it is almost imperceptible came over the onlookers. Shoulders released and eyebrows softened.

Clara turned her eyes downward at her beads, then back up at the officer. Then, stabilizing her crouched body with one hand and swinging with the other, she hit him right in the jaw with her left knuckle. It wasn't a hard hit; in fact, it probably would have hurt him more if the little girl had punched him.

But of course it was enough, and in a single motion he had her hands cuffed behind her back. Clara's whole body slouched and she hung almost sedated in his grip. She looked numbly up at him. But he was suddenly interested in us. I hadn't noticed it while it was taking shape, but the rest of the crowd had gradually filled in around Dragonfly and me as we watched.

The crowd was watching. Everybody was watching.

"Where do all of you sleep?" he wanted to know immediately.

"In alleys downtown," Clara responded alertly with a brisk lift of her sunken head.

He turned to us.

"You need to head back there immediately," he said. "We don't want to see you around here disturbing the peace. Go on, I'll take care of her," he urged us.

And so we did.

We walked with slouched shoulders. We left the boardwalk with one less body, none of us speaking a word of her again.

All silence then, and all silence now, where I am sitting with Dragonfly in the tent, watching his mother sleep. We found her curled up in a ball peacefully biting at her fingertips. Dragonfly is speaking to her softly as rest my chin in my hands, letting the dreariness of his voice lull me.

"Everyone here thinks you're crazy. They don't know, though, that you're better than all them. All of them. They're just a bunch of idiots" He pauses, and shakes his head a little.

He's not saying anything important, but I listen.

He's talking calmly until one of her eyes pops open. He jerks his head back in surprise, and backs away on his knees.

She sits up in terror, clutching the blanket to her chest.

"Get away from me," she whispers throatily.

His eyes plead with her.

"*Get* away from me!" she screeches.

"Help," she starts to yell. "Help! Help! Help!"

Dragonfly turns to me in an instant.

"We need to go," he says to me. And so we both dart out of the tent and sprint across the campground.

We stop only when we reach the picnic tables, leaning on them to catch our breath.

I hear Dragonfly's breathing slow before mine, and I inhale heavily to try to steady my heart rate. He lifts his head to make eye contact with me, and his face is vibrating. He's crying, shaking his head back and forth, and kicking the table beneath him. Finally, he stops his crying, bites his lips, and closes his eyes. When he opens them he looks at me with freakish rage.

"Wanna do something fun?" he says.

I almost laugh, because he is so curiously alive in all the wrong moments.

"No cliffs," I tell him, but it's more of a request. Because we both know if Dragonfly wanted there to be cliffs involved, there would be cliffs involved.

"No," he shakes his head.

He walks over to the ledge, the same ledge the yellow-bearded man had stood next to days ago. The ledge with the money jar balanced on top of it.

I squint. "You want to take more money. For what?"

He shakes his head no again. "I don't want to take more money. Fuck it. I want to burn it."

I take a step back.

"Everybody will wake up. Everybody's gonna know what we're doing. How do you expect to get away with this?"

He smiles. "I don't."

I nervously glance around us. A few stragglers are wandering beyond the fire, but most of the people are put away to rest.

"What's the point of breaking the rules if nobody knows you're breaking them?" he presses.

But then he answers his own question.

"I guess that just depends," he says provocatively, "If you're someone who just wants something to die, or someone who wants to kill it."

I smile finally and pluck the jar off the ledge with ease. Because we both know what kind of people we are.

Entry Twenty

I didn't sleep last night.

I didn't sleep because the whole night we were outside sitting by the embers.

But this time, in a different way.

We were watching the money crisp and curl into black tufts. All of the green turned to a dark dusty black so quickly you could almost forget what green looked like. I found it to be elegant.

I really did enjoy myself.

But Dragonfly was dissatisfied.

Nobody came out of their tents until five A.M., and by that time all of the money had already reduced to dust.

I believe he wanted somebody to inflict rage onto him. He's always looking for more cliffs these days.

Entry Twenty-One

I haven't eaten all that much of anything in the past few days, because I've kind of forgotten to. I used to crave the crispy salmon skin and potatoes that my mother used to make us for dinner, but now I can't seem to remember what they taste like. I don't even really desire food, because the options here range from stale bread to stale bread. But I tell myself that I probably should get to eating some time soon. So I head over to the picnic tables and choose stale bread.

Amber's sitting at the tables when I get there. She's eating stale bread also and playing her triangle with a somber innocence.

Just above her head proudly sits the empty glass jar. I keep side-glancing up at it in all its glory. The stale bread is the humble product of a detailed process of scavenging strategy. Carl and a few others go into town every week and hunt for food. They've found a lot behind the restaurant *Gina's* where the owners dump the old uneaten bread. Every week, they come back with arms and backpacks full of bread.

Bread, bread, week-old, month-old, half-moldy bread. What would happen if our bread supply were to end? The manager at Gina's decides he no longer enjoys their terra-cotta colored walls, and starts to redesign. The restaurant is closed down, and a "Temporarily Closed" sign is pasted on the door. The workers that he hires to paint come from a company of infamous liars and cheaters. The manager doesn't know this because he's a manager of an Italian restaurant with a lot of bread, and he doesn't know most things. He signs all of the forms and pays all of the checks without realizing he's being scammed out of his business. He agrees to pay the workers by the hour, and they draw out their time of labor. This goes on for a long time, and it takes going bankrupt for the manager to realize that they're not actually doing work for him. His restaurant is out of business for six months straight. He plans to reopen when he gets back on his feet, but he's an owner of an Italian restaurant with a lot of bread, and he doesn't really know how to get back on his feet. By this time, his wife leaves him and he goes to live with his parents. He's half-suicidal now (or so he tells himself, but he really just misses money) and his parents let him live with them because they believe he has a real anxiety disorder. Or was it depression? They don't exactly remember, but the subject is much too sensitive to inquire him about.

Gina's is shut down forever, and the next time Carl and his troops check for bread, the lot behind Gina's has transformed into a studio where middle-aged women take Zumba classes and aerobic yoga.

The End. There's the end of bread.

I didn't get any sleep last night.

When you don't get any sleep last night you do things like writing the ending of bread.

I realize I've paused my chewing in the process of writing the ending of bread in my head, and I remind myself to continue.

I didn't get any sleep last night.

Dragonfly strolls over to the picnic tables a while later and asks what I am up to.

I mumble something about bread and tell him to go find his mother.

Entry Twenty-Two

Things haven't been changing much around here. The only thing I can tell you is that they've started to refer to the police officers as *The devil's children* after they took Clara away. I don't know exactly who started it, however I suspect Sal may have been the one to do so out of the boyish recklessness that he often indulges.

I've been side-glancing at the empty glass jar frequently. Dragonfly doesn't ever seem to notice it.

These days, emptiness has lost its usual thrill.

These days it's getting old. It's seeming like a long way until The End.

Now I'm perched on a rock that juts out into the ocean. I chose it because I liked the way it reaches just out to the foamy fingertips of the ocean and the way the water teases the edges of the rock, slinking up to the base, but drawing inward just as quickly. I like the way they communicate, the rock and the ocean. They easily converse with each other all day, usually excluding me.

I have the thought that the ocean loves the rock in a different sort of way than most things love. Quietly but persistently.

In the midst of my writing and observing, I catch a glimpse of a figure advancing towards me. I recognize the shape within a few seconds by the staggered, lurching way it runs. I watch with one hand shading my face, squinting in the sun, as his body grows lager and larger until finally he's planted directly in front of the rock.

His shins slam into the base of the rock, interrupting the communication of the rock and the ocean, sending water sloshing up and down. He's panting, spitting all over, and blinking repeatedly.

He seems to be waiting for me to ask what is wrong with him. I'm not very interested in what's wrong with him. I'm more interested in what is wrong with the sacred space now that he has pierced it. But I ask him anyway.

"What's wrong?" I don't turn my head to him when I say this. I keep my eyes on the base of the rock and the ocean, hoping the rhythm will return.

But he waits patiently for me to roll my head around my neck and face him. It feels like my head alone weighs fifty pounds, and it takes a great effort to turn it.

"My mom's in a situation," he reports. His voice is mild now that he's stopped panting and slobbering like a dog.

I wait for him to say more, but he just shifts where he's standing in front of me.

"Just come, okay?" his voice is still steady, but his eyes are coated with a peculiar kind of uncertainty.

So I slide off my rock with a grunt, taking my notebook with me and writing all this furiously as we walk. Dragonfly walks slightly ahead of me and keeps glancing back at me. I expect him to protest about my writing, but he doesn't.

When we arrive, all I can see is the crowd.

The thick crowd of people. Before anything else, always the crowd.

I wonder for a moment if Dragonfly has brought me here to cluster-- to stand with their shoulders pressed against my left and right side.

This is pointless, I think.

But he hasn't brought me here for that. This instantly becomes clear when I realize that the "situation" isn't the crust of the circle, but what exists in the eye of it.

Dragonfly's mother is pressed face-down against the cold cement between the picnic tables, jaw held open by the pressure.

Above her is the yellow-bearded man, pinning her down with one hand and swinging around the empty glass jar with the other.

She's slurring an array of distorted words and sounds and screams. He is screaming too, but he's articulating.

"Where's the money, bitch?" he's barking over her. She's crying and wailing now.

"Where is it?"

He grabs a fistful of her hair and pulls her face close to his.

"Give it back," he whispers, his veins trembling.

I watch the veins in his neck.

One

Two

Three large veins.

Crackling and popping.

"First there was twenty bucks stolen from this jar. I get up this morning, and there's *nothing left*. And who do I find sitting by the picnic tables all suspicious-like but Miss Psychotic over here?"

Dragonfly is unmoving next to me.

I jump inside my own skin for a second, because I consider that maybe Dragonfly brought me here to pull her out of the circle.

But I don't move yet, because sometimes just by looking at him you can tell when he would do things with his arms if he could.

You can feel him tensely running his hands through his hair or casting them wildly up into the air.

You can tell when he would be gripping your shoulders, or when he'd be wringing his hands.

And as I watch him now, I'm waiting to picture him running into the crowd, peeling off the coarse hands of the angry man and dragging her back inside our tent or maybe even away from here forever. But as I watch him intently beside me all I can envision is heavy limbs dangling beside his hips.

I stare at him with a horrific sense of wonder. If not to pull her out, why am I here?

Slowly, a ghastly realization flashes through his features.

He takes one step back from the mass of people, and looks on in a cautious but glorious awe.

"You told me earlier that taking twenty dollars can do a whole lot."

His face was dark, and his mouth dry. But his eyes, on fire.

"Look at what a whole jar can do."

Entry Twenty-Three

I sat with Dragonfly at the embers this morning, and everything was quiet.

"I'm all torn up," he said out of the stillness. "I want to separate from her. I don't know how. It's turning me into an awful, awful person".

I nodded. I knew.

I took him in for one moment, examining all of it before me.

He looked okay, with the exception of being a little dead in the eyes.

Despite that being a commonality here, somehow it still surprises me every time to see it in Dragonfly. The death always seems so painfully confused and alien sitting in the whites of his. But I guess it's home there now too.

There was something else too.

Something in the air surrounding him today was eerily bloodless. It cradled him in gray as he shuffled his feet beside me at the embers.

I saw it in the way he looked at me, and I saw it in the way he didn't.

I saw all of this in the seconds before I jerked my head away.

I didn't look at him for the rest of the morning, but I didn't have to. Remembering what I saw was enough for one day.

Entry Twenty-Four

Sal and I settled on the picnic tables in the late evening with dinner in our fists. Mine had blue mold, and his green. We each turned a watchful eye onto the sea of tents. Not out of caution or self-defense, really. More out of habit.

It did cross my mind at some point that I should probably go see where Dragonfly and his mom were. But it also crossed my mind that fuck them.

I told Sal this, and he laughed knowingly and lifted his piece of bread my way, as if to make a toast.

Then we sat in the rolling dusk for about an hour.

Sitting in rolling dusk slowly strips you of any real sense of time.

My eyes were adjusting with the sky, and I continued to amaze myself with all the figures and shapes and lines I could still make out in the almost-black air.

I think in a softer way when I'm sitting in the rolling dusk. I think it's the same for Sal too.

Finally, he decided it was time to ask me a question.

"What's it like losing it out here? You're going faster than anyone I've seen in a long time."

And all of the sudden my thoughts weren't soft anymore. They were electric again.

They stopped folding over me in that way I like, and they ricocheted off my skull in all different directions. It took a lot of concentration to pick just one to spit back at Sal.

"What do you mean?" was the thought I decided to give words to. There were probably better options.

"You're living in the trash can of the earth, kid. I'm asking you how it smells at the bottom."

I shook my head back and forth two times.

Three times.

Four times.

"No," I stuttered. "No, I'm not like them. I'm homeless, but I don't act crazy. Like them"

I didn't stop shaking my head back and forth, back and forth.

His eyes traced the outline of mine.

"Yeah, yeah. Show must go on. I know," he said.

I grimaced. I turned my attention back to the homeless camp before us.

Bodies crawling amongst the city of everything without a place.

It was everything in between emptiness and saturation of filth.

Everything in between nuisance to the the world and the purest form of insignificance.

Some nights, I have to believe something will happen here, something of importance.

Some nights, when I watch the eerie bodies crawling until my eyes close, I'm waiting for something to come of it all. For someone to kill somebody or scream or fling themselves off a cliff or something like that.

Every night, the outlines of the bodies carry some mystery to them-- some essence of possibility.

A sick kind of hope.

And every morning, they're just people again. Just people without homes, who reek like rat piss.

Every night it's like an apocalypse here, and every morning it's just the trash can of the beach again. Just like Sal said, just the trash can.

At that point Sal decided it was a good time to tell me another one of my problems.

He shook a trembling finger at me.

"While you're here, though. Part of the trash can. You might as well get to know the other trash. Other than that little boy you always hang around with."

"The people here don't listen to me. If I say something to them all they do is look right through me," I explained.

He smiled. "That's your fault, you know. If you want people to *listen* to you and not just hear you, you're gonna have to start *speaking* to them. Not just talking."

I bit off a corner of the fleshy part of my cheek. I spat it in his direction, but towards the ground.

"What's that mean?" I asked with hesitation.

He was enjoying it too much. I didn't ask for all this. All I really did was sit down next to him.

"You haven't ever really told a story to them, have you?" he effortlessly provoked me. "It's 'cause you don't want anybody to know you're here."

He started to laugh and cough at the same time. I couldn't tell one from the other.

I frowned. It was time to go. The moment Sal starts laugh-coughing at me is the moment that it's usually time to go. But inside my tent, in the middle of the grand trash can, I did think about what Sal said to me. I thought about being equally as terrified of being a ghost as I am of being a person.

Entry Twenty-Five

Observation of Dragonfly:
By, me.
His body gets smaller and smaller until I have to squint to even make a line out of it.
Without arms, that's more than kind of what he looks like:
A line.
I almost wonder if other people on the beach mistake him for a line.
Only a connector of two points in space.
And I almost wish they'd get a chance to see him up close.
But I don't blame them for never looking close enough.
Who would want to take the time
To examine a line
But if they did
They would see that nothing is linear about him.
Like his eyes
Or the shoulder blades jumping out of his stumps
Those parts of him aren't withering away
They're just kind of painful
I swear sometimes you can look at him and just feel pain
Dragonfly is mainly pain
But he radiates it
People who radiate things,
Even pain,
have some fire left inside of them

Entry Twenty-Six

Sometimes I like to climb up onto that tall cliff again and just look down into the blue world at my feet.

That's a lie.

I never do that.

I haven't done that since I jumped with Dragonfly weeks ago.

I should've moved past Dragonfly a long time ago, but for some horrible reason I can't leave him alone.

Here's the truth:

The truth is, there is nothing for me here anymore.

Entry Twenty-Seven

A few things happened last night that I'm going to tell you about now. I can't tell you where I'm writing from, because that would give most of it away from the start. But I can tell you this much: I'm not in the tent, nor am I anywhere near it. In fact, I've finally convinced myself that I've forgotten what it looks and feels like entirely. In all truth I don't necessarily want to tell you this story. But I always end up doing it anyway, telling a story. So here you go:

I was huddled in my blankets on the ground of the tent, trying to wrap them as tightly around me as possible. It was cold that night, with some dampness in the air, the kind of air that makes your nose feel all numb and wet. I was lying there with my numb and wet nose, occasionally glancing over at Dragonfly's sleeping face to check if his nose was numb and wet too.

It was about two in the morning, and I felt like I was the only person awake in the world. I wrote a few things to you in here, but crossed them out soon after because I wasn't making any sense.

Then I sat hunched over in front of the notebook and bit my nails.

I stayed up for hours biting them off, one by one, and spitting them in a little perfect pile on my blankets.

I think I went to sleep soon after I completed my pile.

What I do remember is hearing a loud bang rupturing my space. I remember gathering my senses for awhile until I registered the noise that had jolted me. I remember feeling my way to Dragonfly on the other side of the tent, and shaking his shoulders.

I asked him, "Dragonfly, did you hear that?"

"Of course I heard that," came his voice from the blackness, and he was annoyed.

"Well aren't you gonna do anything about it, Dragonfly?" I shook his shoulder stumps again and again.

He sat up. "Jesus Christ, just leave it alone."

I did do that.

I did leave it alone, until another burst punctured the silence, then a sound of glass shattering, and silence again.

Dragonfly and I sat in the stillness there, staring at the outlines of each other's faces, until I spoke.

"Did you hear that?"

I could feel him rolling his eyes in the darkness. Finally, his voice came quietly.

"I don't want to go out there."

"What do you want to do, then?" I asked.

"I think that I want to sleep next to my mom," he told me shamefully.

He sheepishly kneeled over to the third corner of the tent, and flopped on the lump of blankets. But just after I heard the thump of his body, a gasp came from his chest.

Somewhere between him screaming in my face several times, "She's not here, she's not here!" and me feeling numb and unmovable, and him kicking my limp hands furiously, begging me to move, we ended up standing by the benches in the freezing cold.

My arms ached and itched violently from the biting air. I tried to scratch them, but my nails were dull. I remembered biting them all off earlier that night and regretted it. I remember thinking that my nose was even more cold and wet now, and I hugged my sides and rocked back and forth.

But there was something else that was making me cold from the inside out.

In front of us.

She was spread out on the wet pavement when we saw her; her lips parted slightly; just the way I'd seen her lay in the tent for so long. But in the midst of all his screaming blurred into the moon spotlighting her and the chirp of the crickets, I happened to notice that she looked the most at ease I'd ever seen her.

And for the first time, I realized that she was beautiful—beautiful in a way that I'd never seen in anything before, nor do I think I will ever see again.

I marveled at her heap of a body.

I wanted to look at her liberated cheekbones for as long as I could.

But Sal came up behind me and placed a shaky hand on my shoulder. It almost brought me back from where my mind had wandered, and I heard the loud screams from Dragonfly again. I heard him shaking and crying and screaming and falling apart in front of me, but my eyes still only watched lights: lights of the moon and the streetlamps far away, all little circles of blurry heat blending together.

Finally, my eyes refocused slowly, and I looked down to notice a glass jar broken beside her and a gun tangled in her wiry hair.

"She killed herself," Sal was saying coolly, looking me square in the face.

"She took my gun, and ate a bullet." His eyes were bloodshot, and his face was gaunt. I remember briefly wondering about the vein that seemed to come alive in his neck that I had never seen before.

I thought I heard him murmur: "Thieves are never safe" but I couldn't be sure.

I looked away and noticed a few stragglers of homeless standing around with squinty eyes. Clara and Amber and yellow bearded man and people I thought I knew parts of now ghosts under the magnetic sky. I didn't even try to make out their features in the minimal glowing light, but just watched their silhouettes float around, curiously observing the woman on the ground. They said nothing, or at least nothing that I heard, and meandered back, unmoved by the whole thing, into their designated tents.

I saw the ghosts come and go, and suddenly, looked up to find myself completely alone with the body. Dragonfly had left at some time too, but I can't remember when.

And so I knelt down next to the pile of lifelessness and watched her. Then, I started to speak.

"You beat the game," I whispered to her.

Dragonfly was in the tent, furiously picking up clothes and blankest with his teeth and shoving them into a little drawstring bag when I returned. With each item he smashed into the bag, he pounded harder and harder with all the force of his neck and head. I watched him curiously for awhile, and I knew he felt my presence. Finally, when his bag was stuffed to its maximum, he spun around to face me.

"I'm leaving," he announced.

"That doesn't sound too bad," I said.

And after a moment of silence, "I'll go with you," I decided.

"You're not invited."

"Yes I am," I corrected him.

"You do know what an invitation is?" he resumed pulling the zipper open with his teeth.

"Alright," I said. "Well, *I'm* leaving to go out on the open road. If you want to come, Dragonfly, you're *invited*."

He shook his head a few times and climbed out of the tent. I packed my stuff in his mother's old backpack, throwing in my notebook and some blankets and some stale bread and some clothing. I hesitated when deciding whether or not to take the blanket that had been hers. I took it anyway.

Then I darted out of the tent after him and caught up to him at the crosswalk out of the beach parking lot. A streetlight lit up the air between us, and I yelled into it.

"So, I guess you decided to take my invitation?" I asked.

He didn't roll his gigantic eyes at me this time, though. He just stared out at the ghost city that we were making our leave from. I turned around and stared with him, and then back at the crosswalk, following his eyes wherever they went.
He gazed hungrily at the asphalt in front of him, trying to muster all the strength he had in his body to move one foot off

of the beach parking lot. To cross, to just cross.

I looked at his quivering legs for a long time, and in a sudden gesture lifted my right hand into the air and raised my middle finger toward the camp. Though caked with mud and tar, it seemed to illuminate the small space around us. He burst into a smile, and shook his stubby shoulders with a breathy laughter that came from his chest. As soon as he did, I slowly raised another middle finger *for* him and kept them up. I had two now: one hand for him, one hand for me. Finally, with newfound explosiveness, he darted right off the crosswalk and into the dark street. I sprinted right after him, and we went running through the road, weaving in and out of the lanes, dodging a few honking cars and getting splashed by rolling wheels in puddles on the ground.

We screamed until our vocal chords went raw and we flung ourselves over parked cars and raced around closed buildings and whipped our wet hair around in the glowing streets, all with my two middle fingers held up in the air.

We heard the shouts from store-owners on their nightly shifts, and the screeches of wheels as they spared our lives but we didn't *care*, not in the slightest. And if ever I stopped to look around and take it all in, the only spot my eyes would draw themselves to was the body in front of me whirling itself wildly into the air. And I was back up, up on my feet again, right there with him.

After so long at the camp, it was magical to *just leave*.

Dragonfly's mother had done it: she had just left. Now we could too.

I don't remember much of where exactly we ran that night, or what exactly was spoken.

What I do remember is the way my lungs felt-- the way they lifted me out of my own body.

That night we sank into our little world for what little time we did have, fighting the looming sunrise like it was a disease.

And it was a disease.

Because we both woke up with it, strewn across the sidewalk of a gas station somewhere, covered in mud.

MALIA SIMON

Entry Twenty-Eight

So you know where I am now. I'm at this gas station somewhere with an awful kink in my neck and a shooting pain in my spine. I start to lean on my elbows slowly, but discover quickly that they're far too mangled to rely on. I wipe sticky hair off of my cheeks and squint at Dragonfly's body. I kick him about three times until he yelps a little and sits up beside me.

"What?" he snaps.

"*The open road,*" I say. There's still a lightness in my voice, despite the plague of the morning.

"Are you just going to keep saying that?" he asks. "You said that in your sleep like five times last night."

He starts to kick his blankets into his bag.

He moves in the way of someone whose mother didn't just die.

But it's still on my mind.

You forget most things. Even if they're important.

But there are some things that will never leave you.

Even if you forget how to speak or listen or read, the force of them will always churn somewhere inside you. They will be preserved in a separate compartment of your soul: a place solely for them.

This is one of those things. I don't think I'll ever stop being enchanted by her body.

"What are you doing?" I ask him.

He pauses and turns toward the increasing number of heads poking out of their car windows at the gas station.

"I don't really think we're welcome here," he says.

"That's kind of the point of being homeless," I patiently remind him. "If you can find some place we *are* welcome I'd be happy to hear about it."

I turn to see a gas station worker walking our way. He approaches us and stares us down for awhile, muttering to himself through gritted teeth.

Finally, he speaks to Dragonfly," Young man, who do you belong to?"

Dragonfly just stares at the guy all frozen.

"Hm?"

Feeling a little neglected, I stand up quickly.

"Actually, Dragonfly here," and I gesture to him, "has been unable to speak since birth. He's lost his arms and his voice, and it's offensive to him to be talked to that way."

"I am so sorry. Respect for you, man. I just was wondering if you kids—"

"We kids don't like to be talked to that way. It's insensitive to approach a boy like that who can't *speak*."

I pause.

"We are just leaving now, aren't we, Dragonfly?"

"Yeah," Dragonfly says.

The man looks down, confused, and backs away slowly, fiddling with a cell phone at his waist.

I pack my stuff and wave at the man as we trot off.

After we've traveled a good distance away from the gas station, Dragonfly looks at me with his huge eyes.

"What?" I ask.

"What was that whole thing for? You could've just said we're homeless. He's a gas station worker, what could he have done?"

"*The open road*," is all I say in response, and I run in front of him for awhile after that.

I do run. I run and run and run and run, keeping the mantra of the open road on my leading scent like a hound. My nose to the ground, my chest forward.

But eventually, I lose fervor. Because it's light out now. Oh, sweet pretending, in the dark of the night. Under the spotlights of the streetlights you can pretend you know how to turn your spirit back on. You can pretend it's easy to splash around in the city and remember how to kiss life with a parted mouth. Having a phrase like *the open road;* it's something to fantastically dance around. To run away is brilliant.

But I don't live in the shadows, or dashing between cars, or under the street lamps. I live next to Dragonfly, in the bleak sunlight, with a bag weighing on my shoulders, with a cramp in my spine.

There's nothing like another dead skin cell flap on your lip, hanging on for an hour before it flakes off to remind you of this exact reality. The ugly cracks in the sidewalks, or the sorry state of my hair. Things like that, revealed pathetically in the sunlight, never fail to remind me that I haven't much left to believe in at all. The only thing I believe in is running away. It's the only thing that's proven to turn me out of myself for moments.

And Dragonfly has taught me to believe in one more thing: destroying something new every day. Just destroying whatever you can find. If the first thing in your path be the core of your own existence, so be it. Destroy it anyway. Destroy the shit out of it anyway.

After awhile, Dragonfly catches up to me.

"You know where we should go?" he says.

After a few seconds of silence, he tells me where we should go.

"Hollywood."

I study him for a long while.

"You're good at bad ideas, Dragonfly," I tell him.

"Why?" he wants to know. "There's tons of money to be made there. You just sit there and look sad, and *one* of the ten million people that pass by every day has to give you something."

I fold my arms into my huge sweatshirt. "I don't want to go."

"Doesn't matter," he says. He starts to walk north for a few minutes, and I watch his body morph into the air slowly. Something I could watch all day. But then I call out to him, because I start to worry that the air will snatch him right out of my hands.

"What?" he yells, still a hundred feet away from me.

"I'll go to Hollywood," I say. "I need something else to believe in."

We settle in for the night on the side of the road in some bushes that smell a little bit like licorice and sadness. Before we go to bed, Dragonfly takes out his lighter with his teeth and we light some trash and old sticks and inhale deeply as we watch them sacrifice themselves to flame.

"To the scum of the earth," he laughs, as the whole pile blows up in sparky yellows and reds. I watch his face from across the masterpiece for a long time, my chin settling into a groove in my palm.

He starts chuckling, his shoulders shaking. I watch curiously. His short laughs come at a constant tremor, never slowing or accelerating for that matter.

"Remember those idiotic fucking people?" He says finally. "Remember that blind lady who said she *'saw things'* anyway?" He raises his eyebrows as if to invite me. "Remember that saggy sonofabitch called Sal who tried to be your father? And what about Clara? You think she's dead by now? Or flopping around in the streets like a drunken buffoon, grabbing people's wrists?" He howls. "Idiots!"

"Tell the idiots we're free!" He spits into the fire and it hisses up at him.

I keep my gaze on his cheeks as they relax into concavity again. He'd beautifully lost it, right in front of my face. I am honored to witness his crumbling. He is staggeringly beautiful against the flames, perfectly reflecting everything I love about the night. I watch him with open eyes, not saying a word. We believe in the same things, it's easy enough to tell myself that by the fire.

Finally, I give it up and snort too. My shoulders shake silently, thinking of the idiots. The idiots! The idiots who roamed around; the idiots we left behind to feed off themselves!

I watch with half-open eyes as Dragonfly drifts off to the

smell of plastic burning. He had thrown some old water bottles into the flames.

Entry Twenty-Nine

We did make it to Hollywood. I won't tell you how, because it really means nothing at all. But I will tell you that we walked across these stars on the ground. They're somewhat fancy-looking with names printed in gold at the bottom. The names seem to go on forever, a hall of dead people who probably mean something to somebody.

You walk down the sidewalk and you're bombarded with people: just mobs of people in different colors and sizes and shapes. They're all crowding in like cattle. They stand in lines waiting to get everywhere, and they all have their eyes on something behind them or ahead of them or beside them, but never within them. But somehow, amongst all that, you kind of have your own world that you carry with you anyway. Within the context of so many other little worlds, your own feels more sacred. As I was walking through the clumps of people, I was thinking to myself that the city makes you feel a little bit more beautiful. I was thinking that it breathes something into you, a little bit.

So I was walking, breathing what the city gave me, when Dragonfly just stopped suddenly next to a pole against a building.

This is what he said to me, through teeth clenched to hold his bag:

"Here".

And so we dropped our bags and unloaded our blankets into the new here. And we slid down against the dusty wall. I looked around me for a long time, and looked at all the other homeless people in their other Heres. There was a black man talking to a white man without teeth. They were both yelling.

There was an old woman draped with only a tattered blanket traveling around to the mobs of people, clasping her hands together and showing them small pictures of babies. And there was another white man standing on the corner screaming about God and other threats. And I guess there was us, the boy with the big eyes and no arms and the girl with nothing but the notebook. It would be naïve to believe we could experience any intimacy with our spot on the wall. The prints that our bodies made in the sheet of dust merely covered someone else's from the day before.

When it got dark, Dragonfly pulled out his blankets with his teeth, and rolled over on them. I did the same. We piled our feet on top of each other's and watched the stars for a few minutes of silence. Pretty soon, the preaching man came wandering towards us with white eyes glowing. He collapsed down right next to me, almost on top of me.

"Who are you?" Dragonfly had inched up the wall, his back stiff. I continued to lay down in my blankets, my eyes wandering all over the new man.

"I'm Eddie Albert!" He yelled with a directionless laugh. I remembered the name. I had stared at it on a star on the ground, I remembered.

"You're a star," I said.

"Sure am!" He screamed, and then laughed again.

He wasn't a star, though, and I knew that. He was a homeless man, was all he was.

Dragonfly was staring at him in awe.

"Dragonfly," I said. "He's not a star."

Dragonfly looked disappointed. "I knew that."

"Not a star," Eddie Albert said with a wide smile.

"Go away, you piece of shit," Dragonfly spat. "You're not a star. You're not Eddie Albert."

Eddie just threw his head back and laughed that laugh again. He started rocking back and forth, mumbling to himself, gnawing his thumbs.

I turned to Dragonfly, who was becoming sort of a major ass lately.

"He can stay even if he's not a star."

"He's just another idiot. We need to get to sleep," he said.

But then he turned back around, because he decided he had more to say to me.

"And you know, why don't you ever laugh? Like, ever? All you do is this snorting noise, but you never laugh. You wanna know something? I think you're living in some fairytale world too, just your own weird version of it."

"Your own version of it," Eddie said and clapped his hands.

Entry Thirty

I ignored Dragonfly for the first few hours of the day, because he deserved it. I tried talking to Eddie, but it was near impossible. But then I started thinking about downward drift. Downward drift theory proposes that if you're crazy, you naturally drift downward until you're homeless, not the other way around. It makes sense why all of us on this corner here are crazy. It means this is where we were supposed to be, from the moment it all started for us. It means that I understand Eddie more than I thought I did. I really do. He's a star, and the world is ending, and I understand him.

So I started to talk to him. I went over to his corner in the morning and sat beside him.

"Hi Eddie."

He smiled at me curiously as if we'd never met.

"Did you know that life on Earth will be over soon?" I asked him.

He started to sing a song that said "My girl" a bunch of times.

"Yeah, well, it is. And I think you should know that, especially since you're a star and whatnot."

"I'm Eddie Albert!" He yelled.

"I know," I said.

I looked at the sign next to a bucket out in front of him, and it read: *need money*.

"What are you going to buy if people ever do give you money?" I asked him.

He pulled out a bag of white powder and handed it to me. I

pinched some between my fingers and watched it flake away.

My conversation with Dragonfly back at the wall:

"How was your day?" Dragonfly asked in the evening.

"What do you mean how was my day? My day was homeless. And yours?"

"Mine too," he said.

"You know, Eddie is a star, if he wants to be" I told him. "It's okay."

He turned toward me and smiled a trying smile. I didn't know I could make him smile like that. Or maybe it was the city doing that, just like I was telling you. Either way, he was looking at me like that, and it filled my blood a little bit.

I popped up suddenly. "Come on."

"Where are we going? We just got here," he complained.

"We're going to steal something."

"Okay. Why?"

"Now that we're homeless, we shouldn't be good people anymore," I explained patiently.

"We were homeless before."

"Yeah, Dragonfly, but when you're homeless in a big group, you're all sort of still pretending that you're fine. But now we're *really* doing this. We left the idiots, remember?"

He stared at me.

"Alright, so let's go already. Come on."

He pushed himself up the wall and started to follow me. I didn't really know where I was going, but the direction I was walking felt like the way to steal something, so I continued.

After a while, I led us to a shopping center with stores and restaurants and markets. They were all lit up and busy with heating lamps out front and little menu signs in the windows. They didn't really look like they were supposed to be stolen from. Dragonfly saw that too.

"So what do you want to steal?" I asked him awkwardly.

"Um, I don't know." He started walking towards the grocery store in the center of the buildings.

We made it through the double doors and into the blinding light. Everyone who passed us looked for longer than people normally look at each other.

Dragonfly was looking around him frantically.

"What are we supposed to steal here?" he whispered to me urgently.

But I barely heard him, because I was enjoying the sensation of running my hand along all the loaves of bread. I liked the feeling of the packaging on my fingertips.

"These breads are so squishy," I openly observed. "How do you think they get the breads so squishy here?"

Dragonfly was impatiently scanning the market.

"Has bread always been this squishy?" I wanted to know.

Dragonfly, finally overwhelmed with his own anxiety, kicked out a shopping cart from the row behind us.

This grabbed my attention.

"A shopping cart?" I looked at him.

"Well, what else are we going to steal?"

"I don't know. Not a shopping cart."

Shopping carts are big rolling rectangles that people push on and carry their food in and don't usually steal.

Dragonfly was still leaning restlessly on the cart when a clean man with a badge that said "Harry" on it strolled up to us.

"Hey there, you two. Your parents anywhere around here?"

"Right there," I pointed far behind him, and he spun around to look.

Just then Dragonfly kicked the cart slowly towards the sliding glass doors. By the time Harry turned back around, Dragonfly was almost out the door.

"Young man," his cheeks were puffing with redness and frenzy. "What are you doing with that cart?"

I stepped around Harry. "We're stealing it."

For what I imagine would be standard speed for a robbery, Dragonfly was moving painfully slowly out the doors, and I ran to push him forward.

I jumped on the edge of the cart and rode it all the way out the door and into the parking lot.

"You can't do that!" Harry was yelling after us, but his voice grew fainter and fainter as we pushed farther away.

When we reached the other side of the shopping center again, Dragonfly collapsed onto the ground out of breath.

"How was that?" he asked me after his breathing slowed. "Do you feel like a bad enough person now?"

"Progress," I said.

But then, my eyes started to wander. I was gazing off a little in the distance when something very important grabbed hold of my eyes. A huge downhill not a mile from where we stood stooped below the business centers around us. From what I could see, the road was blocked off by a little white gate with a single chain draped around it. I turned to Dragonfly to see if he was looking too. He was, and his eyes were stricken with fear.

"No," he said.

But I had already made up my mind. I started to push the cart in that direction faster and faster, a hypnotic smile climbing my features. I must have turned into some wild animal right then. I had tapped into a different part of existence that most of us don't even know exist inside us. I saw nothing, but I saw so much. I only saw the hill. Because it looked so much like life. Dragonfly was calling my name, but I didn't hear him, because I didn't have one right then.

I was approaching the crest of the hill when Dragonfly appeared behind me, completely out of breath. I climbed into the cart and looked up at him, imploring his eyes with mine. I looked at him the way we used to, the way he looked at me on top of that cliff back at the beach. I didn't need food or water or a home or anything. I needed *this*. And he understood, though he pretended not to. He turned away, his jaw line quivering.

"You really want me to do this?" he begged.

I just kept looking at him like that.

And so he did it.

He kicked the bottom of the cart. He kicked it, and the wheels started to scrape the ground. The rolling rectangle with me inside of it moved faster and faster across the plane until it dipped down the ledge and plummeted. I felt my stomach merge with my chest, and I screamed with life. Then, I remembered what Dragonfly had said, about how I don't know how to laugh.

In those climactical moments between top and bottom, I can remember my thought process precisely. Within split seconds of fear and excitement, I was able to consider the momentary person I wanted to become.

And so I laughed. I laughed loud enough for the whole world. I screeched with laughter as gravity pulled me faster than I could understand rationally. I was even laughing when I felt the cold impact into my ribs, when I cupped my hand on the dribbling blood coming from inside of me, when I dry heaved into the muddy grass that my teeth bit into. I held my red-coated hands in triumph to Dragonfly on top of the hill, and threw my head back in more brilliant laughter. I lifted up my shirt and watched the openness of my stomach pour out red rain, and I laughed harder.

I looked up and Dragonfly was beside me, wrapping his coat around my midsection with his teeth and legs. He appeared blurry to me, but I could see that he was crying just a little bit. And I remember he was telling me to quiet down. I laughed, but it was softer this time, and it waned away as the blood crusted.

Entry Thirty-One

I woke up this morning, and nothing hurt. Nothing was funny anymore either, but nothing hurt. I patted my stomach and the ruined coat tied around it. I stumbled up to my feet, then fell to my knees and threw up on the side of the road. I untied the jacket from myself and flung it onto the pile of vomit in disgust. I kicked Dragonfly to wake him up, and he shot up from the pile of leaves he was sleeping on.

"What?" He shouted.

"We should go," I said with a distant hoarseness in my voice.

So we hiked back up the hill, and I tried to turn and look back at the shopping cart at the bottom, but I couldn't really turn my core to the left or the right. I wanted to scream, because I felt the emptiness washing over me again, the life disappearing as if it had never met me before.

There is no emptiness inside me, no void. I am inside of it. That is a fundamental difference that I understood as we walked.

We walked up that long hill, Dragonfly biting his lip, me thinking to myself that I would've been a little bit saner today if I'd gotten more sleep last night. The day wasn't going horribly until I remembered that now Dragonfly and I pretty much can't do anything. He doesn't have arms, and I don't have a useful stomach. We can't even be bad people if we feel like it again.

"What will we even do now?" I asked him.

He knew what I meant. "No matter what, there's always more things to break," he said, and his eyes were red and tired. I realized he was right, and it satisfied me all the way back to our Here.

When we slumped back down against the wall, I noticed a curiously long line of homeless people that seemed to lead to nowhere. They were pushing and shoving and hitting on the backs of each others' heads. Everyone wanted to get to the front of the line, though I was convinced nobody knew what it opened up to.

When you live like this, you need lines sometimes.

So we got in line. Eddie was a space in front of us, working on pushing through a big woman. He was carefully pulling back her hair and screaming in her ear, "I'm Eddie Albert!" And she was swatting him away like a fly, looking aggravated but still only partially aware of his presence. I started pushing bodies too, because it seemed like the thing to do. Dragonfly kicked me in the shins.

"What the hell do you think you're doing?"

I stopped my work to turn back at him, breathing heavily with a woman's arm in my hand.

"I'm being homeless," I explained and got back to it. But being homeless gets tiring and, after awhile, kind of disgusting. It's just bodies. Bodies of everyone else who are being homeless.

I was a little bit farther up in the line when I took a break. I spun around in a circle, but I realized that I had lost Dragonfly. I grabbed Eddie and yanked him towards me.

"Eddie! Where is Dragonfly?"

He cocked his head at me with that stupid smile.

"Who's Eddie?"

And he laughed and laughed while I stood there dumbly in front of him. This quickly became his new favorite thing. He paraded up the line yelling, "Who's Eddie?" and laughing to himself.

Finally I surrendered and just sat down in the middle of the line, starting to feel the pain in my ribs a little bit. I touched them with my thumb, smoothing the dried blood. Then I laid down, my hands on my head, and let my eyes fall closed. I felt feet crunch down on my hair and fingers a few times, but I didn't really say anything; sort of just pulled on the roots of my hair until the people passed.

I think that's what you do. You just sort of pull on your hair. You just grip it right at the roots and squeeze.

It was dusk by the time I let go of my hair and opened my eyes, and I looked up to see a thinned-out line. I stood up and weaved through hunched over bodies and sleeping lumps. My hair was wet on my shoulders from where I'd been pulling and biting it. It felt strange and curious to me.

And there, at the very front of the line, was that stick of a shadow. I ran up to him, pushing bodies out of my way. I stopped short a few feet away, and watched.

An old man was feeding Dragonfly; slowly forking food out of a Styrofoam container and into his mouth. Dragonfly would look back and forth quickly, and then lean forward and wrap his lips around the fork. I winced. Because he looked pathetic. He looked like a damn baby right there on the street, and he knew it too. But he had gotten to the point where he didn't have enough energy to care.

I ran over to them and grabbed the fork out of Dragonfly's mouth. The old man started backwards, his hands in front of him.

"Stop feeding him," I demanded. "He doesn't need it. He's not weak."

But Dragonfly turned his eyes into tiny, angry slits. They quivered with red veins, and for the first time, I saw how tired he was. I saw how much he needed to not care that he looked fucking pathetic. I held the wet plastic fork in my hand and dropped it solemnly on the ground.

Dragonfly spit at me, and it hit me in my left eye. I left it there, afraid to move.

He hadn't spit to convey that he wanted to destroy me. I would be honored if I were Dragonfly's next item to destroy. Dragonfly spit on me like I made no difference to him anymore. He cared about surviving and being fed. But he didn't care about me. I shook with jealousy.

"While you were over there beating the living hell out of people, I was getting this! You don't have to take everything I have. You don't have to take everything I have. You don't have to take everything I have…" he said, over and over again.

Entry Thirty-Two

"Hi, I'm Alex Davis. Leader of the church just down the block there," the man said to me.

I had just awoken, and he was waving a shiny flyer in my face.

"Yeah, and Eddie is a star. Go fuck yourself," I said.

"Our church is a place for everyone. We're just a big group of people devoting ourselves to the Lord, and we'd like to bring in some new people who need extra saving."

I looked up from the concrete finally. "What."

He looked pleased to have achieved eye contact.

"You heard me. Anyone. Even the homeless! No, scratch that, *especially* the homeless. You see, our church follows the concept of being "radically inclusive." That means anyone can come. It seems you and your friend are having some troubling times. Feel free to drop by anytime and join us in prayer."

"He's not my friend. He's Dragonfly. Also, I don't pray."

"Not yet." he said. The eagerness in his eyes was intrusively innocent.

"Not ever." I didn't tell him why.

"I was just feeding your friend—" he paused and widened his eyes, and smiled a small smile, patronizing me just enough to make my left eye twitch.

"Oh, I'm sorry. *Your Dragonfly.* I was feeding your Dragonfly and talking to him about our services. He was very interested."

"No he wasn't." I shook my head.

"Actually, he was quite interested! You know, there's

nothing wrong with being interested in the Lord. Especially when you're young and still willing to change"

"There's not enough time before The End for me to change very much at all, though," I mumbled.

"It's never too late to change," Alex Davis said.

Entry Thirty-Three

Today I looked at my reflection for the first time in awhile. I caught my own eye in the glass of a storefront and paused for a minute. My hair, which had once been a light blonde color was now streaked with gray and muddiness. It was wet and matted. My eyes sunk into their sockets, my teeth were yellow-black.

I watched Dragonfly come up behind me in the reflection. He started to stare at himself too, making different faces, tilting his head back and forth.

"We really look like shit, don't we?" He snorted.

I smiled widely into the reflection. "Speak for yourself. I look amazing!" And burst out laughing, cackling and pulling on my wiry, coarse hair. Dragonfly laughed too, and we both got a little more okay.

Lately I've been less okay than usual. But today felt a little different.

"Do you ever think we should try to eat something?" I asked him. "I mean something real. Not just scraps from a garbage can." He looked me up and down, seeing for the first time how visible my bones were.

"Yeah," he said. "There's that church over there. You know they give free food to the homeless sometimes and they have really nice—,"

"No," I said.

He followed me back to our Here and nudged me around to face him.

"Eventually, we'll need to."

I avoided eye contact. "But not now."

Dragonfly was quiet for a few minutes, before saying suddenly, "I saw you talking to Alex Davis".

I continued to avoid his eyes.

"What about him?"

"He told me that—he told me that God sent him to reach out to me. He said he's a prophet. Or something like that"

I cackled.

"Dragonfly, you listen to that shit?"

He shifted uncomfortably. "No, no, not really. I just thought we could try going once or twice. Just to see what it's like."

Entry Thirty-Four

There are some things that Dragonfly and I find we need to stop talking about if we want to survive together out here.

We need to stop talking about food.

We need to stop talking about whether or not Eddie Albert is a Star.

We need to stop talking about *the idiots*.

We need to stop talking about the church. Every time we talk about it, one of us ends up running away. We don't agree, and I don't think we ever will. So we stop talking about it. But right now, I'm just counting down the days until I lose him to them.

I'll tell you about the last best night I had with Dragonfly. And I knew it too. Throughout the whole damn thing, I knew it was going to be the last best time.

We were sitting at our Here, not talking about the growing list of things we couldn't talk about. I was looking at him; he was looking at the lights. There were creatures up and down the block that resembled us in quality of clothing and hair and skin, but we still looked on them like they were wild animals. There we were, saddled together like two of a kind. There we were, together almost every second of the day.

But we didn't see that much of ourselves in each other either. We didn't see much of ourselves in anything.

When all of a sudden, something ruptured our little space.

A pounding bass, across the street.

Pounding

Pounding

Making our ears hurt.

At first we both covered our ears in subtle angst, turning our heads to the ground and muttering to ourselves.

Because we aren't children anymore.

We've done things to ourselves out here that force us into bitter adulthood. We've begun to visibly destroy ourselves. I've come to believe that the moment you start to visibly destroy yourself is the moment you're not a child of the world anymore.

Once you stop seeking to nurse off the fruits of your environment and instead choose to dwindle on your own devices, you can no longer be nurtured by this world.
And so we weren't nurtured by the world; we were just residue on the lives of other people and other things. So the separation from your childhood makes you mutter at a pounding bass. It makes you turn away and shake your head, and agonize over the sound like it's a home intrusion.

Maybe a month ago we would've taken the invitation of the pounding bass and followed it. But not anymore. We scoff at the times they'd pour us our fortunes and we'd lap it up like wine.

Idiots!

Euphoric curiosity is a luxury! We live off crumbs. And we're okay with it, too.

But then

Something sparked our interest.

At an instant the bass grew louder, then quieted, and our heads followed its sloppy trail. We looked to see the door of a night club swing open.

Two filthy drunk women stumbled out of the bar and threw the remains of a bottle of whiskey and a pack of cigarettes into a garbage can. I turned to Dragonfly with widened eyes.

Yes, we were grown now. And no, the sound of music alone couldn't intrigue us.

But the sight of something so potent and infectious as alcohol could set a spark.

And I thought back to the moment on the hill, when Dragonfly told me there's always more things to destroy. This time, I thought, it must be ourselves.

I shook his shoulders by his stumps, feeling the inflections of my voice fly out of control.

"Come on!"

He shifted his eyes back to the garbage can, and the door of the nightclub swinging back and forth. The disc jockey was preparing the people inside for an "old favorite."They were all pretty happy about it, screeching and laughing and clapping. I could see little glasses and big glasses rise up into the air and clink together and spill out a little.

Little glasses

Big glasses

Laughter and clapping

And I wanted to go to that trash can.

Dragonfly and I ran over to it and I sunk my hands deep into its contents. I felt my way to the whiskey and cigarettes.

The loud speakers of the bar played "Sha la la la la la. I was down at the New Amsterdam…"

Dragonfly and I instantly spun toward each other and threw our heads back in excitement.

I held the bottle up to him and his eyes raced as he unscrewed the cap with his teeth. We both knew the song: Mister Jones, and we felt the heat of the club rise even as we existed just outside of it. I could see that bodies were moving together, and people looked happy. Or wild, at least. Dragonfly and I wanted to be happy, or wild at least, too.

So I cupped my hands and washed the whiskey down my throat.

Burning

Burning

And then a subtle warmth.

I watched Dragonfly's eyes light up with exhilaration. I poured some for him too, directly into his mouth, and watched the warmth descend through his body just as it had descended through mine.

I laughed with excitement and held up the bottle in triumph. I poured it down my open mouth, on my face, all over the place as Dragonfly was yelling along with the music:

"She's suddenly beautiful. And we all want something beautiful; man I wish I was beautiful!"

I laughed louder this time, and screamed with him:

"So come dance this silence down through the morning! Sha la la la la la la la la yeah!"

Dragonfly ducked his head, pulled the bottle right out of my hands with his open teeth, tilted his head back, and sucked on it until his mouth overflowed and he had to spit it out. I was bent over laughing hysterically, clapping my hands and screaming about nothing in particular.

I was dancing across the street and back, taking back the bottle from him and having a swig of whiskey in between breaths, confusing it with air every few seconds.

"Cut up, Maria! Show me some of them Spanish dances." We both flung our heads back in the air.

"Pass me a bottle, Mister Jones!" we sang together.

Then we laughed and laughed our lips dry. Each time I felt the warmth slither down within me, the more oblivious of the cold air outside I became. I wanted more, and he wanted more. We were drinking it together now; I was holding it up and pouring it out for both of our open mouths.

"Believe in me! Help me believe in anything, 'cause I wanna be someone who believes!"

I was dumping the whiskey over my head then, whipping my hair around me in some kind of ecstasy. It drenched my ratted clothing, my knotted hair, spilled over my chin and down my chest. And it fascinated Dragonfly. He loved it. He was laughing so hard he couldn't make a sound, his body pulsing back and forth.

I was laughing too, harder than I had laughed even in the shopping cart when my ribs swelled with blood. I was laughing so hard it took me a few minutes to realize I was vomiting. I only knew because I felt a burn traveling in the opposite direction of my throat. I leaned over, then whipped my neck back up and widened my eyes in invigoration.

"I wanna be a lion! Ah! Everybody wants to pass as cats! We all wanna be big big stars yeah but, we got different reasons for that."

We tried to dance, though we were stumbling all over the place.

"When everybody loves me, I wanna be, just about as happy as I can be! Mister Jones and me… we're gonna be big stars." The song finished and the audience inside the bar smacked their hands together.

The glasses clashed and clinked, and Dragonfly and I clashed and clinked our bodies together.

People who swung out of the nightclub walked wide circles around us, but we just stuck out our burning tongues at them and watched them grimace.

Back at our spot on the wall, I mumbled. "Dragonfly. Good song."

"Song? OH yeah. Good." We both fell back onto the wall again in a dreary delirium. Eddie strolled over to us and invited himself to sit down. He started laughing with us, looking back and forth at our fading faces with a big smile.

"Eddie Albert!" he said.

Entry Thirty-Five

I woke up with the taste of whiskey lingering on my lips. It made me feel sick, but I believed it was worth it.

I will say that today I thought about the ocean a little bit. That's pretty much what I do here, is I think about things for a little bit. I thought about how I miss it, actually. I miss the way I could wake up every day waiting for the muffled roaring. But I guess we have our own ocean here. It's the people. There they are every day, making their own roaring noise that's just as dependable as the ocean and blending together in a way that you could get used to. It's easy with large masses of people like that. You don't have to worry about their eyes or the movement of their cheekbones. If you learn to let your eyes go soft, they blend together like that, and they don't seem separate anymore. Just one big smoothie of things; they're almost the ocean.

But if there's one single person that you look at every day, you see their eyes. And you see the way they curse in their sleep, and you see the twitch of their veins every time they try to stand up, even if you didn't choose to. The world just doesn't let you soften your eyes on one person like that. I kicked him to wake him up this morning, and he didn't even jump this time. That's how I knew we needed to do something different today.

"Let's do something different today" I said. I had momentarily forgotten about my understanding from the previous night. Dragonfly and I had already had our last best time. I had felt it then, and I trusted that. But when you wake up, you forget about the insights of the night.

He sat up under his blankets, his back propped up like this little piece of paper against the wall.

"Okay. Let's eat something then," he suggested.

I didn't really want to eat anything, though. Numbness takes away your appetite, too. It leaves you wanting to do something different every day, but ending the day just as hollowed out as before. Nothing different can ever happen if you're numb.

All things that happen in numbness are the same.

I looked at Dragonfly, though, and he really did look like a piece of paper.

He kind of did still look like a boy; he wasn't growing anymore because his body decided to spend more time eating itself than doing other things a body should do. Even his stumps looked too big for his body now. I thought of the way we sang Mister Jones on the street, and how he looked with whiskey running down him. And I started to wonder if there were parts of Dragonfly that hadn't left childhood in the way all of me had.

I began to think he looked very out of place in my world, just the way he did on the top of the hill that day. My world, actually, was sort of killing him.

"You probably need food," I decided.

He looked up at me. He was surprised.

"Can we go to the guy from the church? He gave me real good food," he said.

I was annoyed at him then. "Why are you asking me? Knock yourself out."

He started to push himself up the wall. I stayed put. "You don't want to come?"

"No. I'm numb," I explained. He seemed to get it. Either that or he just really needed food. Because he rushed off to that line again.

That line is there almost every day, with church workers and charity people all bundled up with big cans of wet food. Dragonfly usually ends up at the front of the line, because he has no arms. People like to feed other people who don't have things like arms. It makes them feel good about themselves. It makes them feel like they're saving them from the lack of arms. It's bullshit, though. Dragonfly doesn't need to be saved. He just needs food. That's it.

I decided to go over to Eddie. He was sitting in a group of homeless people this time. They were all swearing and laughing meaninglessly. I sat down in the circle. Eddie patted me on the back and laughed. This old woman with yellow teeth and a scarf wrapped around her neck handed me a moldy turkey sandwich.

The pieces of cheese were a white-blue color.

I stared at it and started pulling on my hair a little bit.

Around me they were all doing things like that-- rocking back and forth, gnawing on some pieces of clothing. I realized that I sort of spoke their language. I was part of their ocean, and I watched it happen too.

I threw the sandwich on the concrete, and the woman twitched both her eyes at me.

"Why girl? That was good good food, was girl!"

I just kept pulling on my hair.

She wiggled her finger at me.

"You, you, you girl."

She spat on the ground in front of me, and laughed with her ugly teeth. Eddie started laughing, too.

They were all laughing now. There were about ten of them around me, laughing like complete idiots.

It made me feel disgusting, and I threw up to the side of the road.

I've been throwing up a lot lately. I got a few looks from passers by as I leaned over and let the vomit pour out, but mostly they just stepped around my body on the sidewalk.

Dragonfly came back and sat beside me. His cheeks looked like more blood was flowing to them. What stood out to me most, though, was that he was wearing a clean set of clothes, and his hair didn't look matted anymore.

"Where have you been?" I looked him up and down.

"The church sort of took me in," he mumbled. "It's not a

big deal."

"It is a big deal," and I felt another wave of vomit rising in the pit of my stomach.

"You can go live with the church if they took you in. Do you want to marry the church, Dragonfly? You can go marry the church. They want to marry you back because you have no arms and they want to save you."

He looked me over with disgust in his clean, shiny clothes. "They're helping me," he spoke slowly. "What the hell are you doing?"

We have this same argument every day, it seems. I want to know why Dragonfly wants to be saved, and he wants to know why I want to hold on to things so tightly.

He doesn't see in them what I do. The rescuer saves the weak from a frightening largeness. The wounded, by allowing for heroism, save the rescuer from a far more frightening smallness--that which is their own mortality and humanness. Heroes are far needier.

We never stop arguing about it. But I don't mind arguing with Dragonfly as much as you'd think. It keeps me speaking another language from the one I fear I've taken to lately; it keeps me from throwing sandwiches in groups like that and laughing and swearing at nothing, and becoming one of them.

Entry Thirty-Six

I have spent some time looking back on these notes, flipping all the way back to the first days I started writing to you. I've evolved, and perhaps you'd agree that I've traveled downward.

But regression is a form of progression in and of itself.

The regression builds in the same direction as any monument, which is upward.

Dragonfly has changed too.

So I was sitting with my back against the wall next to Dragonfly. I was looking back and reading all the old stuff, watching it like a slideshow. Dragonfly was doing something with his mouth. I think he was gnawing at his cheeks, because he kept scrunching his mouth to the side, and then spitting out little white flecks that looked like part of his flesh. I looked up from my notes all of a sudden and turned to him.

"We've changed, Dragonfly. Together, though."

He spat out little white things again. "Why are you telling me? Why don't you tell that thing over there?" he motioned to my notebook.

I snapped it shut. "This thing over here probably knows more about you than you do about yourself." But I was smiling, sort of. Because he was arguing with me again. Later that night when I was sliding under my blankets, I saw Dragonfly push himself up the wall and start to walk in the direction of the church. I sat up and opened my mouth to speak to him.

"Don't wait up," he mumbled, and started to walk away.

"I know where you're going," I yelled back at him, and I knew he heard me. "And I will wait up, you son of a bitch."

Entry Thirty-Seven

It's been a few days since Dragonfly and I have started not doing everything together. When you're with someone for a really long time, you forget that you can do things without them. Clearly Dragonfly remembered that option before I did, though, because he started sneaking off at night. Today I wanted to show Dragonfly I remembered that option too.

So I went on a walk today, just in the direction it seemed like walks should be in. I didn't bring the notebook with me, so I wasn't talking to anyone the whole time. It was nice, I guess. A real, actual silence. After awhile, though, the silence went on for too long and I started questioning my own existence and everything like that. I had to start playing a game real quick to make sure I was alive and stuff. I played a game Dragonfly and I used to play back at the beach, where we'd see people and make up stories about them.

I was walking around the corner when I arrived at the church Dragonfly always goes to. The guy who feeds Dragonfly was standing outside, passing out flyers for the next service. He waved all huge and happily at me, and I wasn't sure if he remembered me or if he waved that way at everyone. He was passing out all these different kinds of papers to the people walking by, and most of them weren't angry about it. They were saying things like "Thank you!" and "I'll be sure to make it!"

None of them said anything like "Go fuck yourself".

The church doors opened a little bit. People piled out. They were all smiling and laughing with each other and talking about things that made them smile and laugh more.

This one family came walking out after the first few people. They weren't really smiling like everyone else, just walking out and talking with each other. There were two girls, a man, and a woman. I wanted to play the game on them. I followed behind them for a long time, slinking into the shadow and curves of the streets. They stopped on a bench to unwrap what looked like sandwiches in tin foil. I thought about crouching down behind a trash can, but then I realized I could sit right there in front of them against the wall. They weren't going to see me anyway. Being the way I am makes me invisible to people in that way; but it also lets me watch them even closer, so the joke is kind of on them.

I started the game. The taller girl had brown hair with brown eyes. I noticed that she was pretty, the kind of pretty that everyone notices. She was much more beautiful than the blonde girl, mainly because of her smile. And she was the sort of person that likes to hug people in the middle of the day and feels most of the way better after long showers and buys her mom scarves for Christmas. She was the kind of person who most people pretended to be.

The blonde girl was also sort of pretty, if you tilted your head a certain way. But mostly, you didn't see any pretty in her. She had her mouth tightened up in this way. She didn't smile all that much. The one thing you could notice about her was this flame going on in her eyes. A lot was going on in there. She wanted a lot, you could tell. She wanted more than she should. And after staring at her for awhile, I thought of Mister Jones, and how 'we all want something beautiful'. I realized that was it: she wanted something beautiful. That didn't make her beautiful, really. It did make her more alive.

But one thing the blonde and brunette girl had in common was the way they would both scrunch up their noses when they were talking or laughing. That wasn't pretty either, exactly, but it was the one thing that connected them, and you knew they were family.

The man looked like both of them. He was losing his hair a little bit. He had this vein on his right temple that looked like a jagged lightning bolt. It etched across the side of his head, and pulsed when he squinted his eyes. A lot was going on in his head, too, but you could also tell that he was okay with himself, more okay with himself than the blonde girl. But less okay with himself than the brown-haired one. He looked like he knew a lot of things about the world; he looked like his eyes had changed from how they used to be years ago. I decided he didn't always have that lightning bolt. He gained it somehow, maybe on the same day his eyes started changing.

The woman was probably the most interesting one to look at. The blonde girl was talking to her as they ate. The woman was looking at her like she was the most special person in the world. She was listening closely to everything that was said, and nodding her head. The blonde girl wasn't the most special person in the world, though, and she knew that. So it didn't feel very real to her. She found it hard to make eye contact. She kept glancing away in other directions and shifting around in her seat. But the woman had a lot to give her and most other people. Most people wouldn't say that about her, probably. Because they start getting used to being provided for by her. She never stops, is what's her problem. A lot of people say that love never runs out. But if you have a lot of something like love and you just keep giving it to people, they stop noticing it. So love might never run out. But love does go silent. That's something the woman doesn't know.

After awhile, I realized I wasn't really playing the game anymore. I was just noticing them. Just watching every detail of them and who they were to each other and who they were to themselves. And I didn't need to play the game. It was pointless, really. I didn't need to make up who they were. I could see it. So I guess I did learn something about people today. You can learn even through craziness. You can learn a lot. It doesn't cure you or anything, but it breathes into you a little bit. I found out that if you look really carefully, you don't have to guess about people. I looked up to tell Dragonfly my discovery only to realize he was off marrying the church or something. Then I started wondering what Dragonfly's actual name was before I gave him one. I wondered what would have been different if I had watched him first, before meeting him. He watched me, I think. That's how he knew so much about me when all I knew was his eyes. I also wondered if Dragonfly was actually off marrying the church or if I just made that up about him too. Sometimes your own separate reality and someone else's sort of fold together like that.

As I was wondering everything, the brunette girl and the man started walking towards me. I turned around to see if anyone was behind me. But, in fact, they intended to walk to me. They spoke with each other a little bit, and then the girl stepped forward and held out a lump wrapped in foil. I looked at it for awhile before I realized she was trying to give it to me.

"Here, we have a leftover sandwich."

The man nodded and I saw his lightning bolt twitch.

Slowly I reached out my hand and took the lump. They sort of waited there for me to say something, probably something like thank you. I wasn't going to thank them, though. If you thank someone it means they're a stranger. And I had really gotten to know them so well.

After awhile they got bored of waiting and turned in the other direction.

"Take care of your lightning bolt," I told the man as they were walking away. And I really did hope he would listen to that piece of advice. They spun back around and looked me over in confusion, then slowly kept walking away. They didn't know it, but that was better than thank you could ever be. It was okay, though. I didn't need them to realize it. I didn't say it for them. I said it for the relationship I had built with the lightning bolt, and the man, and human beings in entirety for those thirty minutes of watching them. And I smiled at their backs as they walked away. Then I threw the sandwich in the trash can next to me and started walking back to Here.

Entry Thirty-Eight

We went rummaging through these big trash bins in an alleyway. Just digging and plowing through all the trash and shit left behind.

I was picking out little things that caught my eye. There's all this brown and black and mold and stuff, and sometimes you see something bright red. You kind of just have to pull it out. Dragonfly doesn't agree with that. He says we're looking for food.

"Are you looking for edible things?" he asked me.

"Yes," I told him. But I wasn't. I was looking for the red things. And the blue things. And all the other stuff that wasn't very edible. I pulled out this yellow plastic car, wiped all the dirt off of it, and threw it into my huge pile. Dragonfly had a tiny little pile next to him; everything was carefully sorted out. He had found the end of a banana, the crusts of a sandwich, and a pizza box with some grease and crumbs left over. He was leaning over the bins and reaching in with his neck, then clamping his teeth down on whatever looked luxurious to him. I was watching in amusement, and finding more red things.

Dragonfly noticed my entertained smile. "You could help, you know. I don't have that many arms."

I pointed to my pile. "I am helping."

He sat down against the dumpster. "I actually eat. I actually eat food. I know you're on this weird thing where you don't really eat now. But I'm sort of looking for food."

I slid myself down the side of the dumpster until my shoulders nudged his stumps.

"How's the church?" I asked him.

"The church is fine. I don't go that much," he said with fluttering eyes.

"Is there somewhere else you go every night?"

He looked at me, and turned his head down. He nodded a few times.

"Okay, yeah. I guess I go kind of a lot."

After a long pause:

"The guy from the church. You know, the guy that was feeding me," he started. I grimaced a little bit, and he knew I remembered who he was talking about.

"Yeah, that guy," he said. "He talks a lot about love. He talks about it every time I go there."

I started rummaging through the dumpster again.

"Are you listening to me?" Dragonfly wanted to know.

"There's nothing else to listen to." That was a lie, though. There were plenty of other things to listen to. I could have listened to the reckless drivers on the road or the homeless people singing about a woman named Mary just around the corner, or the muffled sound of the shitty street performers displaying themselves for money, or the owner of the coffee shop taking out his trash and slamming the lid. But I chose to listen to him. Because as much as he was marrying the church or whatever, he still wanted me to hear him.

"What was the guy saying about love? Tell me."

He smiled at me and started again.

"Okay, so he was saying that there's one love. Like, it's the same love for everyone. That's why everyone is allowed it."

I sort of regretted listening to him then, because I got myself all worked up. It was wrong, that's why.

There's no 'same love'. There are a million different kinds of love. There are more kinds of love than human beings, or cells, or atoms, or anything. Like the way Sal used to sit out and look at the stars back at the beach--that's its own kind of love. Or the way Eddie Albert rolls around and sobs in his sleep-- that's a different kind of love. Or the way that one homeless woman plays her violin every Sunday at dawn-- that's a separate kind of love too.

And there are even little currents of different loves that split out from one larger love. There are love circles and love triangles and love beads. There's silent love, like that woman on the street who I watched for so long. And there's broken love, like the way a tortured dog will still come back to its master. And there's sacrificial love, like the man at the church. So there are different kinds of love, and it really goes on forever.

I dazed off for a moment thinking of this. Suddenly, a flip switched in my mind.

I had the urgent thought that the one thing all different kinds of love have in common is that they're all sick. It's all over the streets and the sidewalks and the buildings. It contaminates the earth every single day. It radiates off of people like a fucking disease. And it makes you want to vomit right there.

Dragonfly watched me get more and more upset. He watched me twist and smash my plastic red things together, thinking about how wrong the man from the church was. He watched me do this for awhile. Finally, he asked me something. "Do you love me?" he asked me, apropos of nothing, in my opinion. He closed his eyes a little bit, because he knew himself too well. He knew if he kept them open he would see the whole answer before he heard it. And he was afraid of that, this time.

"I doubt it," I said.

He opened his eyes and studied my face, then shook his head slowly. He looked dissatisfied with my answer. Not hurt, really, but dissatisfied. We both knew, that's why. I had caught the disease from being a human being for too long. Because repelling against something is being controlled by it even more intensely. I almost needed to vomit right then.

"Well do you love yourself?" he wanted to know.

"Which self?" I wasn't looking at him, just playing around with my pile of stuff on the ground.

He started laughing then and shaking his head. "You're god damn crazy."

And that was it. It didn't matter anymore to him, because I was god damn crazy.

Dragonfly got up to leave the dumpsters, and I got up too. I left my pile of red things behind because I didn't feel like not mattering anymore. I walked back far ahead of him with my arms crossed. I took long strides and avoided the little cracks in the sidewalk that are there for no reason. I started getting angry at the sidewalk, stepping longer and harder over it to show it I was mad at it. It didn't care, though. It just stayed a sidewalk. And I stayed god damn crazy, I guess.

I was still far ahead of him, but I kept looking back at Dragonfly. I kept looking back and wondering if I was his disease.

I waited for him to catch up, because I had stopped being mad at the sidewalk and started thinking a little more.

"It doesn't matter anyway to me either, Dragonfly," I said. "It doesn't."

Then I gnawed and pulled on my hair all the way back to our wall.

Entry Thirty-Nine

So maybe you've been bored with me lately because I haven't really been doing anything. I've been collecting red things and thinking about how bad love is and pulling on my hair, but it's hard to tell if you count that as doing something. So today I did something that I've been doing a lot lately, just not recording it. Because I don't really have to record *everything* that I do, do I? Here is the something that I did:

I passed out today. Passing out is like sleeping for a long time, except for much more exciting and less normal. It's much more of a something than sleeping; it really is. I wouldn't suggest that you try it every day of your life, but you should probably try it at least once. There are probably much quicker ways to try passing out than mine, but here's how I did it: Going homeless and falling into a slow starvation. Dragonfly told me that when I woke up to see his face leaning over mine. He said, "You're starving." Not that I needed him to tell me that. "I knew that," I told him then. Because I did. I had felt it for a long time. I didn't tell you, because I was waiting it out. But I really have felt myself falling into a slow starvation. I'm not hungry, though. Not at all. Dragonfly keeps asking me if I'm hungry. That's because he doesn't know the difference: the fundamental difference between starvation and hunger is that hunger is having the void, and starvation is being inside of it. I can reach out my hand and almost touch the walls of starvation here, but I don't feel it anywhere inside of me. And I'm not starving for food; that's not what's killing me. I'm starving to be out. The End is soon, though; passing out is just a little appetizer that feeds me bits and pieces to keep me alive until then.

Dragonfly keeps saying how hungry he is. Every day he tells me that. He says he gets hungrier and hungrier each day. And I just smile at him. Because when he tells me that, that's how I know he's okay. Because no matter how big that kind of hunger grows, it can never directly turn into starvation. Starvation comes from a different source entirely. And that's the kind of source I have to stop vomiting into him. I really do. The thing about passing out that I discovered is that other people don't really like to watch you pass out. They think you're going to die or something. So I've started privately doing it. I tell Dragonfly that I'm going to find food. And then I go pass out somewhere.

So these days I go around a corner or behind a trash can or something and privately pass out. I stay in my little piece of The End for awhile until I can feel dragonfly's foot hitting the side of my cheek. He kicks me four or five times even after I open my eyes. Then he leans over me and yells something like "What the hell happened?" He causes this huge scene and everything. People walk by and turn their heads. Some people stand there and gather around me. But when they realize I'm not dead or anything they kind of walk away. I get up, follow Dragonfly back to Here, and try to talk to him casually while he ignores me, his lips quivering. We do this every day, almost. I'm writing to you now, and it's around midnight. This is when I usually write to you. The world is very much awake at midnight. Midnight is when things are at least half alive. It gives me something alive to write about. Like the street lights. Or the gas stations. Those are really the things I think you should see. You might not want to see me. You might not want to see someone who passes out but isn't really dead.

Entry Forty

Today I woke up, and I wasn't sure if I had passed out or just slept. That's sort of how it is now. I blinked my eyes a bunch of times, trying to remember which kind of unconscious had had me. I rolled my neck around a bunch of times. I leaned my head back on the concrete just to see two sticks of legs behind my forehead.

"We're going somewhere," he said.

"Why?" I sat up and started pulling on my hair.

Pulling.

Pulling.

Gnawing.

"You need to stop asking why so much," Dragonfly was almost yelling at me. "More happens without why."

I was quiet.

"Why?"

He narrowed his eyes at me. "I'm serious. If you ask why and I tell you why, you'll understand where we're going. And it'll be just like every other day. So do you want to understand where we're going? Or do you want to just go? Because I'm leaving now."

He started walking away from our Here, and I followed him with my eyes for a little bit. Then I pushed myself up the wall and followed him with my legs for once.

"What?" I asked.

Dragonfly slowed his pace and looked at me. "I didn't say anything," he said.

I followed him. "Somebody did, then."

He kept walking faster. He was stepping over the cracks in

the sidewalk, I noticed. His strides were long and fast.

"What?" I almost yelled.

Dragonfly spun around. "*I didn't say anything.*" He had a climbing note of pain in his throat when he said it.

We kept walking, and I kept asking "What?" I never asked why, because it wasn't telling me anything confusing. All it did was say my name. And whisper things.

We were walking past stores and little shops and restaurants and people who didn't have to ask "what" all the time. Dragonfly was looking at those people, and wishing he was walking with them, I think.

He was walking ahead of me until it started raining. Then he stopped and waited for me to catch up. I was pulling on my hair and sliding my eyes across the sidewalk like this sort of type writer. Everything was very saturated. Everything was wrong.

Dragonfly spun around in the rain. I remembered when it rained when we were out on the road that day. I liked watching him back then. I liked watching him be happy. I think I saw all the things he still had left. But now when I watched him, and all the "what's" that hung just around him, I sort of saw everything that was gone.

But that didn't matter. The rain didn't matter. All that mattered was this bubble. I sat in it, scratching my head and pulling strings. I stumbled and sat down on the curb as Dragonfly spun around and around with this big smile on his face. I waited to pass out, but this time I didn't. This time I rocked back and forth, but not because I was cold. I rocked back and forth at the sound of my name.

"Taissa," It said.

I didn't ask what.

"Go away," I said. "Please."

I rocked back and forth. I pulled on my hair. The hair pulling *is* the It. I'm just an item of It more and more as I try to pull it out.

"Taissa," it said.

"You idiot. Who did you used to be? You *idiot*," It spit at me.

"*Idiot*," I said. "*Idiot.*"

I repeated what It said to me like Eddie Albert does. I repeated the words because It said them. It told me to. I wondered if that had been the same for Eddie Albert. I wondered if that's how it all started: if *It* had told Eddie Albert his name, and so it became.

"Idiot," I said.

Dragonfly stopped spinning in the rain.

"Are you talking to me?" he yelled. But he knew I wasn't.

He threw his head back and closed his eyes.

"*Idiot,*" I said.

"*Taissa,*" I heard.

"*Taissa.*"

"*Taissa.*"

"*You—*"

Entry Forty-One

I did end up passing out. I woke up and I was back against the wall. My mouth was all dried up, and my eyes were sealed shut. I wiped and rubbed them for a long time until they opened. Dragonfly was asleep next to me. His clothes were all crusty and dried up from being in the rain last night. I stared at his quiet body for a long time, enjoying it just for myself. His stumps had little pieces of artwork embedded into them. When he was asleep, it almost looked like they were asleep with him, not irritated or embarrassed for themselves like they were in broad daylight.

"What's the time?" I asked a woman who was walking by. She had on tall shoes and an ironed business suit. She was walking fast. She looked like the kind of person who you shouldn't ask for the time. But I looked like the kind of person who wouldn't know that.

"It's nine thirty-four," she answered me quickly, crossing her arms and lengthening her stride.

I decided it was time for Dragonfly to stop being quiet and asleep. I kicked him, and he groaned loudly. The woman turned back for a moment at the sound, then kept walking in her direction.

Dragonfly opened his eyes and blinked at me.

"You woke up in the middle of the night," he said, somehow trying to explain to me how we got back here. "You walked back here after you passed out."

We were quiet. Then,

"I was going to take you to the church to see if you'd just listen for once."

But my attention was divided, because It was starting to talk to me again. It cried and yelled sometimes, but most of the time it was just little sounds of chatter. I sort of liked it there. It's like listening in to tiny conversations at a little restaurant inside of me. The conversation is all very civilized, and it usually involves my name. I didn't realize this last night, but It's talking *about* me, not *to* me. So I don't have to answer It. I just have to listen.

Dragonfly was tilting his head at me.

"It's in your head, Taissa. I don't hear anything. It's not real, whatever you think you hear."

But I knew that. Of course I knew that. I never thought the trees or the walls were talking to me. Who the hell do you think I am? But Dragonfly was wrong about one thing: something being "all in your head" doesn't make it unreal. It makes it so much more real. And even better, it's your very own type of real.

I was very pleasant today, with my conversations to listen to. I've never been so entertained, really. Dragonfly kept looking over at me, wondering when I was going to explode. But I knew I wasn't going to. The little chatter, the little chatter keeps me here in a tight little knot.

Every time It says my name, I pull another hair. By the end of the day, I had this whole pile of wiry hair next to me. Dragonfly ended up climbing into himself in the corner. He was rolled up in this little pile of bones, probably wondering how to pass out like I can. We stayed the whole day at Here. I was fine with it.

"*Taissa.*"

I smiled to myself.

It was getting dark. I was still listening to the same track on repeat, but only one part of my self noticed that.
I looked over as Dragonfly lifted his head slowly. His eyes were all red and droopy. He hadn't passed out; he looked too much within himself for that.

"Taisssa?"

My eyes spun into focus. My name again. My name was being said. But this time *to* me. My name was being used as a way to draw me out, not pull me in this time. That's how I recognized the difference. That splashed something onto my face, and I looked directly into his eyes.

"When is the last time you've eaten anything?"
I looked down. "Dragonfly, I—,"

"No," he stopped me. "Don't. Try to remember. I was thinking about that this whole day. I was thinking that I can't call on a single image of you putting food into your mouth. I'm trying to think about it, but I don't know what it looks like. Tell me I'm crazy."

"Taissa," It said.

I turned to It. "Oh, shut up." It didn't. I did my best to ignore It.

"I think that I ate something on the way back from the dumpster," I finally said to Dragonfly.

"No," he said. "You didn't."

"Stop asking me about it, please," I pulled out some more hair and then put it in the pile.

Dragonfly glared at me. "Stop starving yourself, then."

"Why are you blaming me? We're homeless, god damnit. I can't help it," I said.

I saw a vein pop in his neck.

"Don't waste your breath lying to me, Taisssa. I'm blaming you because look around." He gestured his head to the open road. I scanned our surroundings-- the closed up restaurants and the dimly lit street lights, the street performers packing up their things.

"There's no one else here to blame." Then he crawled back into himself and went to sleep.

Entry Forty-Two

I didn't sleep all last night. When you don't sleep, the days start to lose the lines between them. Dragonfly dancing in the rain and me listening to It say my name seem like they happened today, just a second ago.

But right now, there are chains rattling in my head. I look beside me to see that my pile of pulled-out hair has mostly blown away in the middle of the night. I didn't notice it go. I feel my head; I feel the patches and the matted blood. It's definitely gone, I just didn't notice it go.

Same with Dragonfly. He's not next to me. I push myself up the wall and stumble around the corner. Dragonfly's not there either. I know he's at the church, but I still look for him everywhere else. I walk down the sidewalk for a little bit, running into everything. I crash into a fire hydrant, and then a woman holding coffee. It spills all over her coat and down her skirt. She sort of yells, and then backs away carefully, more afraid of me than the burning water dripping down her chest. I walk a few more steps, and then bump into a street lamp. I fall over right beside it, almost spilling over into the street. Some people are stepping over me; some are stepping in huge circles around me. Occasionally, I feel them step on me, on my finger or my leg, and I hear it crunch before I feel it. I wait to feel it, but it never comes. The feeling is gone, I just didn't notice it go.

Finally, I find a little bit of strength. I push myself up on my elbows just high enough so my hands can reach my head. Then I start pulling more hair, making a new pile since the other one left me. *"Taissa,"* It whispers to me. I listen. I'm doing this, and I'm watching people not watch me. The man in the suit walking by doesn't notice me here. A little girl steps on my pile of hair, but she's not even aware of it. They would notice me if they thought I was crazy, but they don't think that. Do you know why? Because people think screaming and crying is what makes you crazy. They think that crazy is yelling out and slamming fists into walls. But that is the biggest misconception they'll ever have. Screaming and crying is still fighting. Screaming and crying, actually, is the only sign of real sanity. But real crazy, real crazy, is the gnawing and the rocking and the pulling.

It's taken me some time to fully realize that, despite popular belief, crazy isn't what you break. Any sane being beautifully destructs every day of their life. Insanity is much more profoundly what you build. The insane build themselves a castle of their own compulsions, devotions. And they relish in every fucking square inch of it, silently, every day.

The silent lunatics are the real ones. Nobody watches the silent lunatics.

Nobody except for Dragonfly. I see the sticks. I see his legs. They're right by my eyes on the concrete. He kicks me. I look up at him, investing all of my strength into my neck. I'm watching him.

He's crying.

I can see his face from down here. It's crumbled.

Finally, he smoothes out his face.

"You should really tell me next time," he spits down to me.

"Before you go crazy." And he kicks me in the ribs again.

After that, my eyes stay open long enough to see the sticks walk further and further away from my face. He turns the corner, and I know he's going to sit on the wall. He's going to sit there, and he's going to wait. He's going to wait for me to get up. Because when I kick *him* every morning, he gets up. I know what I have to do. I grab on to the street light, and start hauling my body up the pole. Finally, I'm vertical. I lean against it for a long time, and feel my eyes close softly. My breathing goes from heavy to sort of okay. I decide that sort of okay is the most okay some things can be.

So I try a step, still holding on to the light post. I let go of the post, and fling my other foot forward. But my body doesn't know my feet anymore. My body doesn't care. It crumples down again, and I am back where I started. I crawl over to the wall of the building closest to me, and push my back against it. I'm able to stand. And slowly, I'm able to walk. I walk step by step in wobbly strides, avoiding the cracks in the concrete. It seems so strange to me that walking like this, taking smooth, steady steps, was something that knew me yesterday. Today, I was born without it again. I relearn things every day. You have to relearn things every day when you're fighting yourself.

Every step now is okay, and I turn the corner to see Dragonfly against the wall. His legs are pressed against his chest, and his head is down. But I know he's not sleeping. He lifts his head slowly at the trace of my presence even from twenty steps away. I take the twenty paces to him and collapse onto the wall next to him. I roll my head back onto my arms, feeling the patchy spots on my scalp again, this time accidentally. My breathing isn't very free. My legs are turned in on each other. The coldest parts of the concrete are cutting into my back, and I have to twist it around every few seconds. But I look up; I look up for a second. And he's smiling at me through those eyes now. And I remember why I relearned how to walk.

He takes a blanket from his stack into his mouth, and flicks his neck so it falls on top of me. My eyes are barely slits now.

"Taissa," It calls to me softly.

I crane my head out of the blanket to listen to It.

Dragonfly turns and sees me do this, and I lower my head back down instantly. A second later I lift my eyes just above the peak of the blanket and watch him watch me.

Entry Forty-Three

Dragonfly's pile of blankets is empty. He's at the church, I figure, so I grab fistfuls of my hair and pull on them until I see him walking back.

I watch him come closer and closer. My head is still resting on my shoulder, because my neck hasn't decided to come to life yet. And as he is approaching me, I see something peculiar hanging from his mouth. It is a bag, a big brown paper sack. It's swinging back and forth from his teeth like a little sandbag with every movement of his body.

His body comes closer to mine, and I can see now that he's almost running. I'm still laying here with my hair in my hands. My head is resting on top of Dragonfly's blankets. But Dragonfly. Dragonfly is running. Dragonfly is definitely running.

He reaches me, out of breath, and spits the bag out of his mouth. I just sort of stare at it, not sure whether or not he wants me to open it.

"Thanks. For the bag," I tell him.

He's leaning over, panting and spitting all over the ground. He laughs a little bit.

"No," he says. "Open it. You're supposed to open it."

I stretch out my arm from where I'm laying on the ground and pull the bag toward me. Dragonfly keeps on being amused while I turn it around in my hand. It has a little ribbon tied around it. I wonder to myself if Dragonfly had asked them to tie a ribbon around it, or if they just did.

"Don't you want to open it?" he laughs. "You're not very good at getting presents."

I open the bag and stare down at a huge red cupcake in a

plastic container.

I turn my eyes up at him. "You're not very good at giving them." Then I throw it as far as my arm lets me, and it lands just short of the street.

Dragonfly runs to go get his shitty present, and comes back with it in his mouth. He spits it back down at me.

"I don't need your goddamn cupcake," I almost yell at him, and kick it away from me.

"Yeah, okay, I know." He's looking at me like he has a plan. "But you don't have to need it this time. I got you a cupcake because it's full of artificial shit and chemicals and sugar and stuff like that. What you *need* is real food, like meat and bread and stuff. But a cupcake: nobody needs a cupcake. So this time, you can just want it."

I stop trying to reach my leg out and kick the cupcake, because what he said sort of makes sense.

He smiles and nods excitedly. He's thought this through.

He smiles. "And if you just *want* it, you can have it. Can't you?" He's smiling bigger now, because he knows that's how it works for me.

I reach out and grab the cupcake. By now it's all pressed up against the side of its container, and the frosting is smeared all over the place. And I'm not hungry, but I think I want it. I break open the plastic and take a bite of the cupcake, getting it all over my face. Dragonfly is standing over me with anticipation in his eyes. They're lighting up more and more with each bite that I take, and by the time I finish it he's pretty much jumping up and down.

He slides down next to me. "Was it good?" he wants to know.

"Was it bad for me?" I ask him.

"The worst," he says. "There's like, chemicals that they use to make plastic in there. Probably dirt too. And dyes, lots of dyes that are probably not very edible. I don't even think they have a food group for cupcakes."

I lift my head and smile at him.

"You did good Dragonfly."

He grins back long and slow, then turns his head to the street again.

And then we sit there. He doesn't speak a word to me for the rest of the day, but settled into his eyes is something comfortable. I don't believe he even blinks. Every now and then I see his eyes reflect a glare as a car drives by. He'll take a breath, and I almost think he's going to say something. But then he'll just keep staring out past anything I can see. It seems like he is looking at the buildings across the street from us, but I know he is seeing through the walls of those too. You had to be seeing through a lot of walls if you could watch the same scenery right in front of your face for three hours and not get bored by it.

We sit there until the day runs out.

We bathe in the placidity that the day provides, and we never ask for a change.

We sit there until the sun turns everything into its own pool of gold, and then past that. We sit until the sun pushes the gold out of everything through all its crevices, and instead made the scene a light sketch of grays. We sit while the sky plays its story, and the boy who never blinks and the girl who never needs are less than a shadow behind it. And then we sit until nothing is a story anymore, not even the sky. We sit until everything is rubbed with charcoal, and the distant screams of the homeless sing the night.

Entry Forty-Four

Things have been going like that for some time now.
Dragonfly comes back from the church. He brings me
something I don't need. And then we watch the day break.

Today, though, Dragonfly didn't come back with a paper
bag in his mouth. He came back with something else.

He stood right in front of me with his legs spread wider
apart than usual. He looked down at me, rolled over against the
wall. I had the thought that I would look dead to a lot of
people, because I am admittedly more dead than most people.
But Dragonfly knows I'm not dead, so he yelled at me.

"Come on, sit up." He kicked me. "Come on."

I twisted my head around on my neck to look up at him.
His body wasn't wide enough to block the sun from making
me squint like crazy.

"I want you to come with me this time."

"Come with you where?"

He coughed at me impatiently. "The only place I ever go."

I sat up straighter and snorted a little bit.

"You want me to go with you to the church?"

He nodded his head at me.

I laughed in a sloppy way then pushed my chin into my
palms.

He looked disappointed.

"I don't want to keep going alone."

I ignored this useless sentiment.

Then he tried something else. "You think the world is
ending soon, don't you? So why don't you just come with me if
it doesn't matter anyway?"

So I got up. I pushed myself up the wall.

"Okay," I said. "I'll go with you." I was going with him because it didn't matter, not because it did.

We walked side by side for three or four blocks. I lost count. I was carrying all his stuff on my shoulders, because he told me we might want to stay for awhile. I told him that wasn't going to happen, but somehow I ended up carrying his shit anyway. Dragonfly ran ahead of me and called over his shoulder.

"Come on."

I bumped into a street light; I could barely see in front of me with all his stuff in the way.

"Since when do you run?" I sort of yelled at him and stumbled over my own feet.

He paused in his stride and waited until I caught up to him. "Since I had somewhere to go." Then he smiled a little bit and kept running ahead of me.

I wasn't really sure if I was even walking anymore, and blankets were falling down around me every time I tried to move.

"Dragonfly," I called. I could barely speak.

"How will I know when we get there?" I breathed.

It was silent, and for a long time I thought I'd lost him to his race.

Then, "You'll know," came from just a corner away. And so I kept moving.

And then, I knew.

The double doors that were cracked open just enough so you could see inside if you climbed to the top step. And the marble arches. And the stained glass windows with yellow and blue and green and red in different pictures that I couldn't understand. And the man handing out flyers right in front of the steps and shaking everyone's hands. And the homeless. The homeless sitting on a wide staircase at the throat of the place. The homeless being handed out bread and meat. And cupcakes. And they weren't Eddie Albert or any of his species. They were just homeless. They didn't have piles of hair next to them or matted heads. They ate their sandwiches and they thanked the people who gave to them. They sometimes shook their hands or sang to them. None of them were missing arms, and none of them only ate cupcakes and other stuff they didn't need. They were just blank-faced, peaceful people without homes.

I was standing next to Dragonfly in front of the church, on the top step, not moving a muscle. And not because I forgot how to this time.

I gestured to the homeless and the doors and the sandwiches and to us.

"Dragonfly," I said. "Don't you realize where you've taken me? We don't belong here." I started to walk down the steps, but something radiating off of him made me turn around. I turned around because I could feel that from behind me, he was smiling.

When I let myself look at him from the bottom step, he was smiling even wider.

"Wanna bet?"

And the double doors opened.

Inside there were just about a million rows of benches with different types of people. There were black people, and white people, and young people and old people. But still, only one armless person.

A few of the people saw Dragonfly when we entered and clapped and threw their heads back in some sort of bliss. The people were in the middle of a song about Jesus the Savior. I looked at all the faces. They all stood with their heads slightly bowed, their hands clasped, and their eyes shut tightly. Their mouths all moved to the same rhythm. They rocked back and forth. Their heads vibrated at the same pace.

The song ended, and all the eyes opened at the same time. A tall white woman with thick hair of ringlets moved to the front of the stage. She said a few words I couldn't hear, but it didn't really matter anyway.

No matter what she was going to say, they were going to clap. And they were going to dance. And laugh. Because they didn't come here to find anything. They didn't come here to learn, or hear. They came here to sink in.

Bliss.

The room was saturated with bliss.

Dragonfly's face next to me began to look like the thousand others. I blinked at him, trying to remember what he looked like on the street just minutes ago.

"Welcome to our afternoon service," she greeted them all. They clapped at her.

"Stand up if this is your first time coming here," she said. People scattered around in the audience stood up, and you could tell they were sort of embarrassed with themselves. But the people next to them patted their backs and shook their hands. They were proud of each other, and themselves. I watched it and felt a little bit diseased. I moved further back into the safety of the doorway.

The woman clapped her hands at the crowd this time, and they loved it. Then everybody started clapping at each other, and nobody even knew what they were clapping for anymore. Everyone pretty much forgot what clapping was anymore; they just enjoyed the sound of smacking their hands together. She looked out into the audience, scanning the heads. She was looking for someone.

"Fairly often now, we welcome some of the homeless to join us for our services. We have food drives and toy drives every Saturday for the homeless who make their camps on our staircase outside."

She was still searching the crowd. Dragonfly was next to me in the doorway, and he started turning pink in the face.

Finally, her eyes landed on what she was searching for. I noticed she kind of pretended not to notice his stumps, and I decided I hated her for it. She wasn't pretending his arms *were* there; she was pretending his stumps weren't, and it disabled him even further. I hoped he didn't like the way she carefully ignored his stumps. I hoped he hated it too. But he was beaming right back at her.

Her face brightened and she pointed to the doorway where we were standing.

"Every week, we get the pleasure of being joined by this lovely young homeless boy." Dragonfly stepped back into the doorway, embarrassed in front of me. We both knew he wasn't young and lovely and homeless. We both knew he doesn't give people the pleasure of his presence.

But then she was looking right at me. She was speaking to me, softly and slowly. The room energy was shifted onto me.

"This boy has told our church a lot about stories, and why he values them. He's told us that you have a story. He said your story is important. Would you mind sharing it with us?"

I pulled on my hair and blinked a few times.

She smiled at me sympathetically. "Your friend has told us so much about you." I looked at Dragonfly. He nodded.

And I finally solemnly, sadly understood something.

This place, these people, the sandwiches and the staircase is all Dragonfly's notebook. And just like I'll put him in mine if I want to, he'll put me in his. So I didn't have to tell a story; the place already knew. The walls have breathed me more times than I would've liked, but I had no choice in it all. There are no doors here.

I looked at Dragonfly and shook my head back and forth, and I knew he wanted to say sorry. But he couldn't say sorry, because the people were watching him, and the people don't think putting someone in your crazy world is something to say sorry for. The people here think putting someone in your crazy world is saving them.

The woman lowered her head at us. She was watching us look at each other and knitting together her eyebrows.

"So, Taisssa. Are you up for telling a story?"

I pulled on my hair.

"I'll tell a story," Dragonfly yelled out. He brushed past me and walked up to the front of the stage. He walked slowly, and the people at the end of each row pretended not to look at his stumps. Then it kind of became a contest of who could pretend not to look at his stumps the most.

He stood at the microphone for a long time. Everyone waited, and no one asked why he was standing at the microphone for such a long time. Everyone just watched him stand at the microphone for such a long time and pretended that they had the ability to give him time. They pretended that they all possessed time and space, and that they could just pour it out into the room if he needed to be provided for.

But Dragonfly knew he was melting time that nobody could give him back. So he started talking.

For a split second, he looked at me the same way he did when he was about to jump off the cliff, and then I lost his eyes to the crowd.

"This is a story," he said. "It goes like this:

A lot of people think that my mother randomly went crazy. One day she just woke up and turned the corner. Well, it was never like that. My mom was always crazy. That's something a lot of people don't know. I'll just start off by saying that. We used to drive out along the windy roads about half a mile from my house. The house I had before I didn't have one anymore.

One day before we left to go driving, I asked my mother if she had taken her pills. The ones the doctor gave her so she would be okay every day. She told me she didn't need them, and that the doctor could stick it. Then she grabbed her keys and took me driving. We were about twenty minutes in when my mom started yelling about something. I asked her to calm down, and to pull over. But she kept yelling. She was saying, 'I see him, I see Dale'. Dale was my father. Dale left us five years before that. But she kept yelling that she saw him in the road. At first I thought she saw him lying on the ground in the road and was trying to avoid hitting him. But after awhile, I realized that she was seeing him running on the road, alive. And she was trying to run him over. She kept pressing on the gas and spinning in and out of the lanes. She kept yelling 'I'll fucking kill you, Dale! Don't you run from me, boy!'

The last thing I remember was reaching my arms over to the wheel and trying to grab it. And a loading truck, and a lot of glass. I remember that too. And then I woke up in the hospital. The first thing I asked the doctor was whether or not she was alive.

The first thing she asked the doctor was whether or not she had killed Dale. And I remember reaching out to grab a glass of water on the side table. Except for, I didn't. Because I couldn't reach out anymore.

The doctor explained to me that both of my arms had been crushed when the car flipped over. He had to amputate them. Have you ever had a dream where you want to scream, and you know how to scream, and you could scream as loud as you could, but you just can't scream? That's kind of how it is. Or how it was, at least. After awhile, I stopped having the urge to reach, or to scream. And I just stopped trying to get things. And I forgot what it felt like to want to touch something, or to grab it or to pull it in. I started to make myself into someone who watches things.

A bunch of people with cameras and notepads were waiting for me when I left the hospital; they wanted to know about the crash, and they wanted to know who was the hero: my mom or me. Everybody always wants to know who the hero is. But I just told them that we were accidentally alive. That's how I felt for the next few years. Accidentally alive. Even without my arms, I took up more space in the air than I wanted to. And so I ran away to join the homeless camp on the beach far from here. But my mom found me awhile after that. Not because she was looking for me. But because she had run away too, and we both had nowhere else to go than that shitty place. I'm not as different from her as I had thought."

The woman in heels slowly started to clap for him, as I whispered "The end" under my breath.

She took the microphone from him, and put a hand on his back.

"I'm so glad you've been able to find forgiveness in your heart for your mother."

Dragonfly nodded uncertainly.

The woman clasped her hands together and shifted them around.

"Well, let's all just look to God for this boy."

Dragonfly's eyes were cast off into the crowd.

I was staring up at him with wonder. Sort of smiling at him. But it took me awhile to realize that he wasn't looking for me. Nor was he looking at the woman, or the people in the benches. He was looking at something outside of this room.

He was looking at his God.

The woman ended the service and Dragonfly practically sprinted out of the double doors. He pushed past all of the people with his torso, and none of them even yelled at him. I followed him out, chasing him down the steps and the sidewalk.

"Why are you running?" I called out after him. He didn't answer me. But finally he stopped running and sat down on the curb.

My breath was heavy when I caught up to him. I was laughing a little bit.

"You believe in all this, don't you?"

He glared up at me from where he was sitting.

"Believe in what."

I pointed at him, still stumbling around.

"In God. You believe in God, and religion, don't you?"

He started to drag himself up off the curb.

"Let's just go," he said.

He walked a few feet away from me, but I yelled something at his back.

"We live in different worlds, Dragonfly. But neither of them are Earth. And that's why I get you, you know? That's why."

And I meant it too. Because here's the thing: a lot of people say you criticize what you can't understand. But I think we criticize what we *can* understand, in the deepest recesses of our souls. So the people in the church make me want to vomit every second I'm in it, but only because I live their disease too. Devotion, bliss, devotion, bliss, desperation. Religion. I understand.

When two crazies converse, they're often blind to their own relation to each other, each feeling saner than the other. Each feeling scared of the other's face, only because it looks so much like their own.

In this situation, we aren't. Dragonfly and I do live in separate insanities. But they're both just as deranged. That's why we've coexisted for so long.

He turned around. He was smiling and rocking back and forth on his heels.

"So, can we stay here? For just a night maybe? Can we stay on the staircase?"

"I already put our stuff down there," I said.

And he started running again, but this time he jogged in place right beside me. He was happy at me. And I guess that was nice.

By the time we had set up everything on the fifth wide concrete step on the staircase in front of the church, the sky was almost all the way coated black. We looked like little shadows right there on the fifth step. Dragonfly had laid out all of his blankets the way he wanted, even though doing it with his mouth took hours. I just put down a blanket and laid on it and didn't help him with his at all.

I sat there and thought about how being strangled is what gives you your voice. So Dragonfly was able to speak at the church today; so I'm still able to write to you, every day. It's what we do.

I just watched him after that, seeing the blankets rise and fall right in front of my eyes. And I was thinking about what he told them. And I was thinking about how many times I had asked him to tell me how he lost his arms. And I was thinking that the church probably thinks they know him now. Because I used to think I needed to know how he lost his arms to know him. That had to be it; the grand story that would reveal him. But I think the second you stop asking to be told the story, you finally really hear it.

Someone's story isn't what they choose to tell you, or how they describe the road or their old house or the way their arms got crushed under a car. Their story is what already exists in the air around them, all that they can't help but carry with them everywhere they go.

I smiled to myself under the moon then, because I decided it was okay that the church had gotten him to say it before I had. Because they needed to hear him say it, and I didn't. That's the difference. And that's something I'll always have that they won't.

And while he is quietly and comfortably unconscious, I am curled up inside my blankets, anticipating the night that I know I will be awake for. He starts kicking in his sleep and muttering words to himself. He's off somewhere inside himself, feeling other places and things and textures in his dreamland. But I am only here, on the fifth step.

Entry Forty-Five

I woke up this morning and Dragonfly's blankets were all neatly made up. I tried to lift my head up, but half of my body was on the fifth step, and half of it was dangled over onto the fourth. I pulled myself up on the stairway and rocked back and forth a little bit, pulling on my hair. Dragonfly was already gone.

I kind of stumbled up the steps, and then remembered how to walk by the time I reached the top.

When I pulled open the double doors at the top of the church steps, the choir on stage was already in song. The head woman was wearing a new set of tall heels and pencil skirt. Everyone looked all clustered together on the pews. I scanned the crowd for the one person who was always a line. Then I saw him, in the very front row. I hesitantly moved away from the doorway and sat down next to him. He nodded at my presence, but didn't look away from the stage.

The people on stage stopped dancing and making noise and the woman took the microphone.

"Welcome, everyone," she said.

She closed her eyes and clasped her hands together on the podium. "Now, if you could all join me in a silent prayer to our Father."

Dragonfly didn't clasp his hands together, because he didn't really have hands. But he did close his eyes and rock forward. I looked behind me and in front of me and all around me. Everyone was closing their eyes and rocking forward like that. Everyone talking to their own God.

I thought then of maybe describing God to you, and what it

is, but I realized I already had been. This whole time, as you watch me tether myself to insanity, you've been allowed to witness the most profound devotion to a God. And the nervous habits and the rocking forward and the pulling hair: those are the prayers. Those are the little sacrifices; those are the chunks of ourselves we cut out and feed to our God, just because we think it's saving us. But the only thing our God is doing is sucking more and more out of us until there's nothing left.

I would never say that God isn't' real. God is the surest thing to be in everyone's life in one way or another. But I will tell you that God is the furthest thing from goodness or purity or cleanliness. God is the heart of insanity. And the prayers are the little scraps that feed the beast who wants the heart of our true being dead.

And my religion, hearing "It" and pulling my hair over and over again, and theirs are one and the same. The only difference is that they're still pretending they're free.
All these people, meeting over their own tombs, throwing their limbs inside of the ditch, and clapping and smiling, giving their life to one thing like I have.

Dogs love chocolate even though it kills them.

All these people, begging on their knees to lap up the poison. Because oh, it tastes so good.

And so I sat there at my place on the bench, pulling my hair as they rocked back and forth and whispered to themselves. And we all prayed to our Gods. We all slowly killed ourselves in front of each other, and we clapped and smiled about it too.

And then, we lifted our heads.

"That was beautiful," the woman said. Her voice had turned into butter some time throughout the prayer.
I looked around. Everyone was lethargic.

Dragonfly finally looked at me. "Did you pray?" he wanted to know.

I looked down at the pile of pulled-out hair on the bench next to me.

"Yeah," I said.

Entry Forty-Six

This morning Dragonfly was sitting next to my body eating a sandwich. That's the first thing I saw when I woke up. Just his knees squeezing the food together while he hunched over and sucked it into his mouth.

He looked over at me as soon as my eyes opened.

"Good. You're awake," he said.

"Why is that good?"

"Because the church is having an early service today," he told me. "They're handing out food to all the homeless people outside of the church doors at nine, and then they're having a service. You should go."

I fell back onto my blanket. "I thought you said it was going to be good."

But I still ended up in the church at nine right by Dragonfly and the rest of our kind.

The woman on stage proposed we do something new that day. She said everyone was to come on stage and profess a part of them they struggled with, and then hand it over to God. People shuffled up the stairs and leaned over into the microphone one after another.

"I've suffered from two kidney diseases since I was thirteen, and Father, I dedicate my life and trust to you."

Clapping.

"I have struggled with an eating disorder for three years and counting. God, I pray that you'll guide me through this."

Clapping.

"My father died last month, God, but I trust you make everything happen for a reason. God I trust you to lead me in my life from here on out."

Clapping.

Then, a face I recognized. Alex Davis, the man who fed Dragonfly in the line and told him he was a prophet of God. I took a good long look at him as he stood above me on stage, and I realized he didn't look like much at all. I wondered if he was numb too. I was interested.

"As many of the kind members of the church here know, I've suffered from depression and bipolar disorder for most of my life. The church taking me in has helped me tremendously, and God I pray that you keep these pure hearts in my life, and I'll keep doing your services down on earth for you God."

Dragonfly was shocked next to me.

The rest of the crowd was quietly surprised too.

Alex Davis, the prophet of God, the vessel of bliss, was depressed.

They wondered, but I knew.

He's strives for nothing more than to be God.

Don't you think God's lonely?

Everybody clapped. I sat still.

Dragonfly nudged me, but I didn't move.

I couldn't clap for him; it would be like clapping for myself.

Somewhere from feet above me on the stage, Alex Davis's eyes met mine, and he shook his head back and forth slowly with a cold grimace.

When the service ended and we were all filing out the doors, Alex Davis spun me around by the shoulder to face him. I tried to turn away, but he held on tightly.

The majority of the people had left to go receive more sandwiches; even Dragonfly was making his way back to the steps and didn't seem to notice my absence.

Alex Davis held my gaze for a few seconds, then spoke sharply.

"What are you doing here?"

I didn't have an answer for him.

"You reek of atheism," he said.

I was taken aback.

"In my dreams," I said. "Maybe if I were free. Check your nose. Smell again. Do I smell free to you?"

Alex Davis loosened his grip. He was perplexed.

"I get you," I told him. "I'm in it too."

He backed away from me, his hands above his head.

"Your mind isn't in the right place," he was telling me.

"Exactly," I bit of a nail and spit it in his face.

I turned to leave, but just before I opened the door he must have spotted the matted patches on the back of my head.

"You've got—you've got some dried blood on the back of your head," He said nervously.

I turned around and grinned a toothy grin at Alex Davis.

"So do you," I said.

"Glad to see you've come to our church!" I heard him yell as the doors shut and the people entered again.

That night Dragonfly laughed a brilliant bubble of a laugh. He did it when he saw a little girl fall on the street, but still, it was a laugh.

I wrote it down in here that he laughed. I considered leaving it out, but things like that are the only things that pierce the constant dimness. Things like that are some of the only things worth writing down. I told Dragonfly that.

"Your laugh is one of the only things worth writing down," I told him in the darkness. Things are easier in the darkness. I decided that I wanted The End to be in darkness. In the last moment of my life, the blood of the night won't be dried on my face as long as there is no morning. It will run out in a stream of velvet; it has to.

Dragonfly was silent after I told him that. He had never been told anything like that before, I don't think. And I also suspect that maybe he has forgotten how to respond to me altogether.

Entry Forty-Seven

Around here the days don't matter much. It's the nights that carry me. But even then I'm moved only by pretending. Today when I was sitting on the fifth step, Dragonfly came walking up with a paper bag in his mouth. He spat it down onto my lap with terrific aim. It was a sandwich.

I threw it down the staircase and resumed pulling my hair. Biting my cheek.

"I bet that stain right there is from some homeless person vomiting up their food," he laughed, nodding to the imperfection on the staircase.

"I bet that black mark right there is dried blood from some fight or something," I pointed to it on the sixth step.

"Or that's just gum," Dragonfly said and we laughed.

"Hey," he said. "I bet we'll leave all these random stains all over the fifth step, and when other homeless people make their camp here, they'll make guesses about it too. Funny, isn't it?"

"Yeah," I said. "Unless we don't ever leave the fifth step."

He stopped chewing.

"Really?" And he smiled this exhilarated kind of smile.

"I was thinking we should do that too," he said.

I pretended to look for stuff in my bag.

He stood up. "I'm going to church. Want to come?"

"No," I said. We do this every day. He says he's going to church, and asks me if I want to come. I say no, and wait for him to come back and tell me about the amazing stuff they did. Blissed out.

I watched him go up the staircase that seemed like a mountain to reach the church doors. I watched him get smaller and smaller. He has grown, though, since we came here. Eating

all this food has made his body want to help itself.
   He has grown taller and thicker, but to me he's still a line.
   I pull on some more hair, because Dragonfly is still a line
and I am too, and life on the fifth step is so fantastically sad.

Entry Forty-Eight

I'm not on the fifth step anymore. I don't think I will be anytime soon, either. This morning I left the fifth step for good, and I'll tell you why. Dragonfly doesn't like the 'why's, but Dragonfly isn't here. Maybe you like the 'why's, so I'll tell you in case you do.

Last night, I was laying under my blankets with my eyes half-open. I was sleeping, kind of, when suddenly, just below the staircase, I caught glimpse of a shadow. It wasn't a stable shadow or one that presents itself with cohesive darkness. It was a sloppy shadow. It probably didn't even know it was a shadow, or that it was projected on the bottom of the staircase. It just stumbled all around aimlessly until I sat up in my blankets and walked toward it.

I felt this need to talk to the shadow, to meet it at the bottom of the staircase and explore it. That was the nature of my trip down the staircase.

It wasn't until I reached the bottom step that I realized the shadow belonged to someone I used to know. Eddie Albert was carrying it. I reached out and touched him on the shoulder. He spun around to face me, and the first thing his eyes were struck with was terror.

Then he started laughing. But I backed up the stairs then, because the terror hadn't left yet, it had just made room for hysteria. As I backed up, Eddie Albert cocked his head at me, a mad confusion twitching in his brow line.

By that time, I had almost backed up onto the top step, but he was coming up towards me faster.

And then he swung a hefty arm and, with a hot grip on my neck, slammed my head and body backwards. My body easily surrendered.

I felt the back of my skull hit the door as if I were knocking, knocking, on the double doors.

He grabbed my arms and flung them behind my head, swinging his fists at me. They struck my face one after the other, with more force each time as he regained his coordination. At first I only knew I was being struck because of the blood that drained from my head down the rest of my body in ten little rivers.

Little rivers of red.

But slowly, slowly, I felt his knuckles. I really did. It was a strange thing for me; I didn't expect to feel them buried inside my own numbness.

But I did. And it wasn't like a sharp knife; it wasn't being stabbed or having skin broken open. His knuckles were like a butter knife stabbing and stabbing and stabbing, never with a simple easy slice of me. A butter knife puncturing through layers and layers of numbness until it reached the ripe inside. It wasn't until that moment with my head against the door of the church that I believed that everything has a core. Everyone has something more to be beaten out of them.

The butter knife kept coming and I was drifting in and out of consciousness. At the moments when I was joined with my conscious mind, I noticed Eddie Albert was crying and screaming. He was trying to ask me something. He was screaming "Who is Eddie Albert? Who is Eddie Albert?" And he was gripping my bloody body as he yelled it into my ears. He punched my ribs a few times, and I felt it in the same spot I had damaged at the bottom of that hill. He kneed me in the side, and that time I rolled my head to the side and vomited all over my cheek. I choked on my vomit a little bit too, and then tried to swallow the burning back down.

My hands pooled with the velvet red I loved, and I could *feel* everything so acutely now. I could feel each skin cell being punctured and opened and poured out. My eyesight was blurry; I blinked and all I could see was dripping red, red, red.

And I wished then more than anything to go out this way. I

told you before that I want to go out with the luxury of the night. I want The End to meet me with the silkiness of the dripping red, not the crusted-over numbness of broken ribs.

The last thing I remember was him gripping my face with both hands and shaking it. He was laughing maniacally and screaming, and I was limp. The only direction I could turn my eyes was up, and he was leaning over me. His face was the only object of matter I saw or knew in the few seconds before consciousness slipped from me too.

And as the nature of all wishes goes, The End didn't come that night. It refused to give me the gift of closing in on me at the perfect time of beautiful destruction.

My mind reentered my body again when it was morning.

This time I was met with another face floating over me. It was the woman from church, leaning over my body. When she noticed I was blinking, she leaned in closer and held my face in her hands. And even though her hands weren't course and blistered and clenching, they still gripped my face with an abrasive strength. Even though her breath wasn't stained with whiskey, it still poured over me. And I couldn't have any of that.

So I pushed her off of me with renewed strength and stood up on the steps, tripping slightly.

I thought of the night before, and how it had felt like I was dying so quickly. It was this place; it had to be. I began to think that being a part of someone else's delusion kills you quickly. Existing in your own is what prolongs your pulse. Living in both is what tears your two selves apart. And that's when I knew I couldn't stay at the church anymore; I couldn't live in two delusions. One was enough.

So I took this body that had been pounded down in the night, and I carried it somewhere it belonged.

I took it down to Dragonfly on the fifth step, to tell him my revelation. All those days I didn't know how to walk, all those nights I crawled on the steps because of my weakness, exited through my pores like sweat. I had some sort of strength, if only for these moments of escape.

I think that maybe your body always reserves another source of strength, on the off-chance you decide to run away again.

I reached out and touched Dragonfly's sleeping head. Blood rushed to his face instantly and he sat up, startled.

His knees flew up to his chest instinctively and he backed up stiffly on the step.

"Taissa. What's going on?"

"It's morning," I explained.

He shook his head, more awake now. "No, why are you all bloody?"

I turned my head toward the church doorstep. "My body almost reached The End for a minute."

A vein bulged in his neck.

"What the fuck are you talking about, Taissa? I don't have time to try to figure you out right now. Why are you all bloody, and why can you walk normally again? Spare me the game, and just tell me something real."

"Eddie Albert came and beat me up. Remember him? He bashed me in. He really just bashed me in."

Dragonfly widened his eyes. "You serious?"

I nodded.

We were silent for a while.

Then finally, I asked him something hoarsely.

"When are we leaving here?"

"Leaving," he said softly.

"We are leaving, right?" My voice was even quieter now.

I looked at him beside me. His body and pulse were working well together. They didn't even have to wonder about letting go of each other. Holding on together was just a system they had. With that I saw that he wasn't a boy anymore. The boy that, weeks ago on the beach, had gone to see the real version of Snow White only sat faintly on his brow then. The energy he carried had filled out into something stronger. It had transformed into something that I couldn't stand against anymore. When I had carried my body over here, I felt certain that we would leave together to find a new Here, just like we always do. But looking at him then, I questioned it for the first time.

"*We're leaving...*" he repeated to himself quietly, learning the words for the first time, feeling their strange shape in his mouth. He breathed out a short breath and shook his head. "No," he said slowly. "You're leaving."

And so I did. I didn't pick up my things on the step. The only thing I picked up was my body and the notebook. And I did go.

But Dragonfly and I both knew that even though my presence was moving away, he was the one who was leaving. Now, I'm laying on a grassy stretch in the middle of the road away from there. It's taken me a long time to get here, and even this far away I can still taste Hollywood on my lips. I'm hoping that tomorrow I'll start to forget what it tastes like. I'm hoping, but I'm not hopeful.

It's gray now in the sky. I'm alone, except for you. And Dragonfly's alone, except for the church. If I'm being honest with you, I only wish I had asked Dragonfly one thing before I left.

Sometimes a song will play on the radio so many times and you're not even listening to it; just kind of subconsciously absorbing it. After some time, you know all the words of it, and you don't even care about it or feel it.

You've just been surrounded by it, and you end up unwittingly taking it in. You take it in to your skin, because after long enough, we end up taking every useless thing into our skin that floats outside of us. We just do.

But then there are songs like Mister Jones, ones that you can exhale out of your lungs while whiskey runs down your back or laugh maniacally along with, ones that have a heartbeat. There are songs that house you or draw a new universe with every word, so many universes you could live in a new one every day for the rest of your life.

So then distinguishing between the two.

You know the words to it, you know it well. But do you live it? Or have you just taken it in? So the one thing I would ask

Dragonfly, before he made his decision to stay with the church is this:

Which song are you to them, Dragonfly?

I have an aching feeling that if I had asked Dragonfly that question, I would have left the staircase with more than my body and the notebook.

Entry Forty-Nine

I've been at this same spot for the last few days. Waking up, starving more, falling asleep. Waking up weaker, falling asleep at ease, waking up weaker again.

I didn't really create a Here for myself.

Tonight, though, I was just sitting in my grassy spot working on the natural breathing my lungs had forgotten how to do.

I watched a man playing a guitar solemnly across the street. Nobody was watching him except for me, but he wouldn't have noticed if they had been. His eyebrows knit together in that earnest way as he sang each line softly to himself. I was watching him, and I got to thinking that we spend too much time and energy crediting our Gods for being creators.

We are creators.

We are.

Everyone has their art.

Art is when you create something that is bigger than yourself.

And we've all created something like that. That's something I can leave here feeling sure of.

So I was just sitting here thinking to myself and trying to remember how to breathe in the normal way when these three women staggered up to my spot. They didn't seem to notice me at first. They were talking only to each other and laughing a little bit. As the cars drove by and the headlights shone on their foreheads, I picked up on bright blue and pink colors swiped across their eyelids and their heavy, long lashes. Two of them had jet black lines across their lash line that made them look like tigers. I took interest in this for a while and sort of remembered how to breathe again.

They each had long, drowsy laughs that rolled off their tongues in a heavy way and fell flat on the way down. They stood in a close circle and nodded their heads every so often. I noticed their voices didn't have any rhythm.

Purposeless.

They were standing on the edge of my grassy area, straining their necks at each car that passed, waving a hand sometimes. Two of them dangled cigarettes from their right hands and tapped them every few seconds. I wondered if they even intended to smoke them, or if they just liked tapping them. Wondering about that brought me back to my own mind a little bit, and I started having trouble breathing again. I let out a little dry cough, and one of them turned toward me with a small smile.

"Who are you?" she asked me. When she was looking me directly in the eye, she didn't look like a tiger anymore. She looked kind of old; her skin was strained and stretched just below her eyes, and the dyed yellow in her hair was trying really hard to be blonde. I felt a little bit sorry for the yellow in her hair.

"I'm homeless," I told her.

She walked over to where I was sitting and placed a hand under my chin. Her nails were freakishly long, and her knuckles were as tired as the yellow in her hair.

"Huh," she said. "Would you look at that."

The one with black hair stopped tapping her cigarette and pressed it to her mouth.

"She's a homeless girl. What's there to look at, Wendy? I swear, you get strange sometimes."

"Haven't yuh ever seen a homeless girl?" The other blonde one wanted to know.

Wendy waved them off. "Nah, nah, this one was watchin' us."

The black haired one laughed her heavy laugh and coughed

a little.

"You're a little paranoid, Jesus Christ."

Wendy didn't seem to hear what she said. She walked around me a few times, and then picked up my hand.

"Go 'head. Tell me about you, what you got going on over here?"

I kept trying to breathe.

"Go 'head. Tell me."

I was able to suck one full breath in.

"I've been homeless for a long time now. I won't be homeless for very much longer," I told her.

The other blonde one suddenly took an interest. She pointed to my notebook sitting beside me.

"What's a homeless girl got to do with a notebook?"

"The world is ending," I recited. "That's why I won't be homeless for much longer. I write everything down in this." I was about to tell her the theory behind it but I couldn't remember exactly how it went. I wracked my brain. I couldn't quite remember…

Wendy laughed. "If the world is ending that soon I'd say I've done a real shitty job with the time I had." Whatever ounce of air there was in her laugh dropped at the last word. I realized she was still holding my chin, and I backed my head away from her touch.

All of a sudden I heard *It* calling me from across the street. I jerked my head around and followed the noise robotically with my body. The three of them watched me with a certain amount of fascination. I was about to step into the street when Wendy grabbed my wrist.

"Come back, darling," she said.

I shook my head and pointed across the street. I *needed* to follow the sound. Sometimes I'm able to drown it out, to sit where I am and cross my arms against my knees. But other times, it's like a second kind of survival instinct to walk into a street or off a cliff or into a car or something else. I believe in death instinct, no matter what anyone says.

The need to spill our own blood.

And here, survival instinct and death instinct aren't separate things anymore. I *need* death to survive. I seek death out of my last grasp for nourishment.

When Wendy grabbed my wrist just before the street, she wasn't just a tired woman with dark liner in the corners of her eyes. She was the obstacle in the path my instinct was directing me.

I needed to follow the voices, I needed to be with them.

I tried to claw her with my hand--tried to bend it out of hers and reach her eyes. But her grip was too strong.

The black haired one was yelling, but her voice came in whispers.

"Let go of her, Wendy."

"*Let go.*"

"This girl is bat-shit crazy."

"We need to get out of here."

But Wendy didn't let go. She just kept fighting me and fighting me until I had drained all of my strength. It didn't take long. I fell to the curb and ran my fingers tightly through my hair again and again, pulling hairs out by the handful. Wendy sat next to me on the curb. She didn't touch my face anymore. She just watched me. I grew self-conscious and turned away from her, but kept pulling at my scalp. My back was hunched over in the opposite direction and my head was down, but I could still hear her voice. It was heavy, but this time in a way I could understand. She wasn't laughing like that anymore. It was my language.

"I was homeless before, you know," she said. "We all were." I looked up slowly to see the blonde and black haired girls stepping cautiously toward me and whispering to each other.

"How long ago?" I wanted to know.

"Not long enough," she said. "It'll never be long enough for me to forget. Bein' thrown around by the world like trash, like a piece of trash." She was talking more to herself than me. I knew this by the way her fists balled up, her nails digging into her palms.

I tugged on my hair.

"Wendy, let's go," the blonde one said.

The black haired one held her watch up.

"We have to get back. Remember?"

It was strange to me. It had been so long since I had been answerable to time. I forgot what it was like to have to be *back somewhere*. I was always just *somewhere*. I lived in estrangement from the prospect of time, never arranging myself through its design.

I guess I have been answerable to The End. But I don't see it as a form of time, rather the opposite of it. The End is the anti-time. That's what makes it so fucking desirable.
Wendy didn't know about the anti-time. She lived on the terms of time. She glanced up at the watch, and remembered that. She pushed chunks of the sad yellow hair behind her ears.

"Right, right. Sorry."

The other two were already halfway across the street when Wendy picked herself up to leave.

"Why aren't you homeless anymore?" I called after her.

She turned around, but didn't answer me.

Entry Fifty

The grass below me
Hurts my back.
It intrudes on my space and I want to get away from it.
I can't.
Pulling out more hair, more hair, more handfuls.
It calls me. I want to go to *It*, but I don't have the strength
to move. I apologize to *It*.
It doesn't forgive me.

Entry Fifty-One

Why don't birds do anything other than pick at things on the ground with their little beaks and flap around?
Don't they know how to do anything else?

Entry Fifty-Two

I waited for Wendy and the others to come back to my area, and it wasn't until tonight that they came to me. I was half-asleep on the ground when I heard their voices arguing in the distance.

"...the best spot, night drivers come by here, you know that."

"Wendy I told ya I didn't wanna go back here to that crazy girl, I told ya."

"I got a real bad feeling about this, I'm telling ya."

"Will you shut up, Norah? This is what we hafta do."

I was too exhausted to lift my head, so I waited patiently for their bodies to come into sight. From the ground their legs looked especially long and orange.

"Wendy," I called. I was pathetically glad that she had come back to see me.

Wendy looked at me on the ground, then back at the other two.

"*Come on,*" Norah said and motioned her in. She glanced back at me and then at them.

A small black car rolled by the grassy stretch, and the girls waved slowly, shuffling from side to side in their tall shoes. The car drove around the area once, then pulled over on the other side. They walked in a line to where it was parked, and I watched the door open for them. Slowly, they climbed in, heels first.

Wendy stayed behind.

She sat beside me on the cold curb, hugging her knees to her chest.

"Where is your father?" she asked me.

"My father?"

"Where is he?" she repeated.

I couldn't speak. My mouth was numb. I shut my eyes for a second, biting off corners of my inner cheek that were still intact.

I opened them, and Wendy was gone.

"Wendy," I called out.

Blankness.

My mind drifted.

I found myself wondering what Dragonfly would think about the two girls climbing into the car, and suddenly felt myself shivering under the cold air. I had been sleeping without blankets for a while now and hadn't really noticed anything. But tonight, I could almost feel my bones crack with ice beneath my surface. I felt a drop of water fall onto my nose, and then more, and then more, and then more. My dry, ratty long sleeve shirt became a heavy washcloth clinging to me. I realized after some time that it was only making me colder, so I pulled it over my head and wrapped my arms around my chest.

I looked down at my bare ribs that poked out of my sides and felt them with my fingertips. They were sharp and brittle. I couldn't stop feeling them.

I realized that I have become a bit of a freak show. I really have. But something about all this struck me as kind of beautiful, it really did.

Even though I am miles away from the church, I feel more in a church than I ever have before. I am on the open road, yet somehow so confined by this steeple that is my ribcage. The voices that greet me here religiously every day are the sounds of the bell that rings on the top.

Strength can be nice to look at. But weakness is far more

beautiful. Crumbling down to the hands and knees, just folding over yourself there like a piece of soft clay. I've seen strong people before; I've seen people with power. I could tell you about pretty people I've seen, like the girls who are all dressed up on Friday nights, the girls who step over my body with their heels. I could tell you about all that. But all I want you to know about is beauty. This kind of weakness is the best way I can describe beauty to you.

My teeth are chattering now, and my arms are shaking together, but somehow I feel at ease.

My naked body curled up in a ball gives itself to the rain and cold.

Dragonfly is gone, the fifth step is gone, the beach is gone, the real church is gone; I only have this one now.

That which was once so painfully something is now so wonderfully nothing again. Everything has breathlessly settled back into ashes.

Entry Fifty-Three

Art is made of the tie between war and freedom.
But the tie between war and freedom doesn't always make art.
Sometimes it just makes shit.

Entry Fifty-Four

Time bore its heaviness on me during the day, and it wasn't until night time that Wendy came to visit me again. This time, she wasn't with the two other girls. It was just her. I noticed the blue color on her eyelids was gone. She was wearing loose sweatpants and an overcoat which she wore pulled in tightly around her body.

She approached my spot in a hurry, snapping her neck to take short glances all over the place before she sat down next to me.

We were quiet for a few minutes. Urgent not to let time take advantage of me, I spoke.

"So, that's why you're not homeless. You sell yourself to men, don't you?"

She looked at her tennis shoes. "Only way."

"Is it?" I asked her. "I'm not doing that. I'm doing it another way."

She looked me up and down. "How's that working for you, kid? Sorry to be the one to tell you this, but you don't look too great."

I shivered. "Doesn't matter. The world is ending. Do you know how soon? Very soon." I'd said those words so many times. It barely felt like I was speaking. I looked at Wendy to make sure I'd actually spoken to her.

I had.

She was smiling sadly at me.

"Okay," she said softly. "Sorry I forgot."

"It's okay," I forgave her.

I still wasn't satisfied, though. I wanted to know why she had to sell herself.

"Why do you pick being a whore over just being homeless like me? Is it really that much better?"

Her head was angled toward mine, but she was looking through me and past me.

"You know, it's rough. Won't say I don't hate it. But it's like this: you know how a lot of people are terrified of flying on airplanes, but very few are afraid of driving in cars? Even though the risk of a car crashing and killing you is way higher than a plane. You know why? Because with people, at least we're driving the car. Even though we're more likely to get killed, we feel better doing it with our own hands."

Strangely, the darkness of her voice was a lullaby that night. It rocked me until I was half-asleep. Maybe it was the beauty in weakness that I told you about before. Wendy was sort of weak, and so she was always sort of beautiful.

"You get me?"

I got her.

Entry Fifty-Five

    I swatted at my face.
    Fuck. Ow!
    Swatting.
    Nothing's touching you.
    Breath. Breath. Heavy breathing.
    Someone's breathing.
    Looking around frantically.
    Oh.
    Oh, it's me breathing.

Entry Fifty-Six

It seems as though it's been a long time since I've seen Wendy. I'm becoming afraid that I won't make it to The End. The days are shorter; I'm only up for a few hours; the rest I'm half asleep. Every night, though, I wait up until the sun goes down, just to see if Wendy will come stumbling out of the trees like she had before.

I've had no luck, until tonight. She sat down next to me as if all that time hadn't just gone by, and I greeted her with an uncontrollable desperation. I began to pull at the tangles in my hair. I felt her fingers land on a matted bald patch.
I closed my eyes. Slowly, she placed her hand back on my head.

"I'm leaving, kid," she told me suddenly. "I've got to do my job somewhere else— can't get enough business around here anymore."

I nodded.

"Sorry to leave you like your father and mother did.

I snapped my head up. "How did you know that?"

Wendy was gone.

Entry Fifty-Seven

I wonder why I'm still alive. It doesn't make sense. I can't help but wonder if I've even made it at all.

If a tree falls in the forest and no one's there to hear it, does it make a sound?

I'm living but no one's there to feel it, am I really still alive?

My existence has lost awareness from other beings. Every existence begs only for that.

Entry Fifty-Eight

Pins and needles, pins and needles.
The back of my arm.
What are these bumps?
Wendy, come back. Please come back.

Entry Fifty-Nine

I'm still breathing out here. I really am. I don't know many things anymore. Faces are hard to make out. But I did know one, when it came right beside mine and looked me in the eyes in the same intrusive way that it always does.

I inhaled a huge breath, and took all my strength to call out, "Dragonfly. Dragonfly. Dragonfly."

His eyes were filled with tears.

"Please tell me you're not dying," he begged. "Please."

I laughed sloppily. "Don't be crazy. I still haven't finished."

He grimaced.

I blinked repeatedly at his face. "How did you find me here? I'm out on the open road here…I'm…"

"You're only about one quarter of a mile away from the church," he said, and sort of chuckled again.

I glanced down, embarrassed for myself and my spot on the open road.

He reached into his bag with his mouth and pulled out a box of pills and Band-Aids and other fluids.

My eyes widened.

Pills

Pills to nourish me

Pills to save me

Pills that I needed

Pills to kill me

I tried to scoot away from him, both hands guarding my face. "Don't give me any of those.   Don't give me anything."

"I stole this stuff from the store down the road. The man caught me, but I told him I had to go save someone's life. So he let me go with it. And now, I don't want to be a liar."

I tried to scoot away from him on the grass.

"Don't do it Dragonfly," I screamed. "Don't do it."

"I've come to help you, Taissa," he told me.

"Why?" I asked desperately.

"You've been talking to imaginary voices here for too long," he told me.

I shuddered.

"Hey Dragonfly, fuck you," I said. "She's real. She was really here."

But talking to him felt so dramatically real, a dark line against the sketches I'd been living for the past few days.

He was crying. Real human tears. But he wasn't weak, so he wasn't beautiful.

It was painful to watch him.

I cried out in pain and reached out to touch him.

"Don't cry, Dragonfly."

"I'm sorry," he whimpered. "All I want to do is bring you home."

Entry Sixty

If only I could tell Dragonfly what I want to say.

What I'm saying is, every word you speak is a contribution to the artwork that is yourself, so don't go smashing your brush on the canvas.

Don't say shit like you said last night, is what I'm saying. Don't fuck it up.

Entry Sixty-One

I woke up today and asked Dragonfly how long I'd been out.

I knew I'd been really sleeping for the first time in a long time.

I never ask him stuff like that, but the world seemed a little different today, a little clearer. My lenses had been soaped up and sharpened, it seemed.

But when he told me five days, I could've killed him.

"Dragonfly, I barely have any time left. You wasted my time. You wasted my god damn time," I spat at him.

He was sitting with his back against a tree. He didn't care that he wasted my time.

"Your time to do what? To die?"

I glared at him.

All I could think was that I hated him.

Drunk on rage.

Drunk on hating him.

"You look so much better," he said.

Dragonfly thought he had given me the pills this morning. But I spit them out when he wasn't looking.

He tried to save me. That fucker.

I smiled at the thought that Dragonfly could never save me.

"So what, now you're going to leave again? Back to the church?"

He shifted uncomfortably. "Well, no. I'm going to stay here

now. With you."

I waited for him to tell me it was only for a few days, that he'd be going back soon enough. But all I got was silence.

"What happened there, Dragonfly?"

He shook his head. "Nothing happened. But I belong here."

I touched his face with my cold fingers and smiled at him the only way I remembered how to. I didn't even mean to; it just came out of me. He gave me the same look back, but as a gift.

"The world is ending, Dragonfly" I said. "Do you believe me?"

He sighed a long, pained sigh. "I believe you".

And I let my head flop gently back onto the ground where I was laying. I had done it.

"The church isn't for you," I told him sloppily. "You know?"

He knew.

Or he didn't.

Dragonfly doesn't always know.

We get settled for bed on this patch of grass in the same way we had on the fifth step— he with his backpack as a pillow, me with a blanket that he brought me wrapped around my body in a cocoon. We say goodnight, but I stay up long enough to watch him sit on the curb with his head between his knees and sob.

Entry Sixty-Two, 9:00 P.M.

The End came faster than I could go fully insane, and for that I was thankful. My head buzzed from the minute my eyes shot open in the pitch black night. I was electric. I was not scared of anything. There was readiness running through me.

I still heard the voices, though they were distant then, primarily because I'd lost interest in them. I'd lost interest in where they intended to lead me— across a street, off a bridge, through a river. I only had one priority then, and it was The End. The only thing that's been constant this whole time.

There are variables in this equation. Time, People. And then there is the constant.

The constant is always The End. Just like Dad intended. All of the small bits of self-destruction kept me on this track, but only at The End could I hope to complete it in earnest.

Dragonfly was sleeping soundly in the grass. I glanced over at him, my eyes scanning all the way across his limbs. He had gotten taller. Older. Nonetheless, if I squinted hard enough, he was still Dragonfly. Just as I met him on the beach that day.

But I realized something as I was scanning his person. Out here, in my middle of nowhere, he was only *my* Dragonfly. He was only Dragonfly to *me*.

Here's the last thing I'll ever learn:

People should talk about the things they love more. Their eyes flash and brighten in this sort of way; their cheekbones glow a little. It's the only real pure thing there is.

I know this because I saw it just the other day. I saw it when Dragonfly was talking about the possibility of being without me.

He had said "I would never just leave you here. Never. If I were to just leave…" and it swept across his face.

It left within a millisecond of when it arrived, but it lived there for a second and that was enough.

Something about his face will always have me, even on a day like today.

Now that he believes me, I knew I was supposed to write him the same note that my father wrote to me and pass on the fatal mission. But here's what I did instead.

I tore out a piece of paper from my notebook and took out a pen of deep black ink, and I pressed the paper hard against the earth.

And I crouched down on the pine needles and broken leaves and did the best thing I'll ever do in my life.

Here is what I wrote:

Dragonfly,

You are the one thing that got in the way of my mission again and again. All the rest gave me the gift of its insignificance. You were the only one who never gave me any gifts. But I don't regret it. You did save my life, though not with all those pills and medicines. (I never took those. You couldn't pull that one off. Sorry.) Because life isn't the way our body survives. You saved my life on the beach that day when you looked at me and told me I had nowhere else to be but where you were. Then you took me there. Our life is the somewhere we have to go. At least, mine was. But now, it's not about life anymore for me. It's about The End. I have to do what I've always had to do. And you need to know that it was never a duty made for you. Maybe not for me either, but I've given too much to it to indulge that thought. I decided long ago that I would always be right about myself. But you're different. You can still make life out of the saddest and most ordinary things. I believe you can still see the city as a snow globe. You've never been set to create one self, and therefore you will never be one to destroy it. You can still be held by the base reality that wants to soothe you. Those are things only you can still do. The church sucked some of it out of you. There's no use in telling me I'm wrong, because I'll be gone before you can argue. But there's still something left deep in your belly that they couldn't take, that I couldn't take. I can't apologize for them, but I'm sorry for the ways I tried to rob it. And you know that I tried. Misery loves company, but I am not miserable anymore. I am just here. So now I'm telling you to leave. You need to go. Go back. Now. Go back to the beach. Go back to stories, to the people who said "The end" every time you finished speaking around the fire. You were wrong. You don't belong here, in my world. You belong somewhere you exist. I named you Dragonfly, and I made you mine for these months. But now, whatever your name is, go. And don't let yourself become somebody's ever again. You really shouldn't have done that.

And that time I knew I'd never see the way his eyes look glancing up at me after reading it. But for the first time, I didn't need to. It was enough just to know he'll be reading it. And I think that's the best I'll ever get.

Now that I'd taken care of my most important duty, I ran down the street. I ran, my arms flinging wildly around me, my feet pressing off the slippery pavement. I was not sure whether it was raining or I was crying, but either way I was delighted by the feeling. I ran, and I ran, and I ran.

My muscles brought me all the way back, all the way back to Hollywood, and from there back to the beach. I lived these past months in reverse as I ran through it all, and it was exhilarating.

And finally, from the homeless camps at the beach, I ran back to my home. My home that seemed to have navigated me back to its core.

Somehow I feel it wasn't purely the power of free will that brought me back to my childhood home. I'm not talking about fate either. I wouldn't try to convince you of that. I'm talking more of a betrayal of codominance, from my unconscious to my conscious.

My unconscious needed me here against the input of my conscious, so there I was. At the door of my own household, flinging myself inside. Everything was rotting and peeling. The countertops were lined with mildew. The couches were crusted over with a yellow-brown substance. It smelled of dampness and sourness. It smelled almost of Band-Aids. The windowpanes were caked with thick layers of dust. Flies and other bugs twirled around different spots of the room. There were heaps of blankets on the floor with potato bugs crushed underneath them.

I paced slowly through the house, an emperor suddenly. I found my reflection in a dusty mirror in the bathroom, and smiled hugely at myself. My teeth had browned. My hair was matted with dirt and blood. My ribcage looked just as sharp as it felt within me. And I was finally alive.

I moved on to my bedroom, kissing the ground as I entered it. The clock was ticking, and I want you to know that I felt no disgust, no waste inside of myself. Dragonfly was free. Perhaps the only real purpose we have is to set each other free.

Unfortunately for me, I only have myself.

I was fucking full of madness. But I was going to be free. That's what it takes to be free when you only have yourself.

And I pulled the old shotgun out from under my bed where I hid it after slipping it out of my father's lifeless arms months ago. I reached for the notebook next to it with the bullet still attached, the tape just barely hanging on. I loaded the gun and I lifted it with a newfound ease that rocked me almost to sleep, but not all the way. I faced the barrel and smiled into it with buzzing eyes. I was overjoyed.

Don't act like you didn't know this was going to happen. You knew it had to be done the whole time. It wasn't about The End for you, I don't think.

You like the other things.

Not me. I never cared for them anyway. I fell in love with The End.

Perfect.

Brilliant.

Beautiful.

Perfect.

Because *that* was finally it. I'd never needed anything until then. *That* was my moment of need, saved up like a single silver bullet.

I was there. I won. It was time to bask in all of my prizes.

But staring into the eye of the gun, my hands went stiff.

It's lonely here at the top. Here at the pinnacle of my life's career. It doesn't matter who you started doing it all for.

Don't you think God's lonely?

Made in the USA
Columbia, SC
23 September 2017